"A marr[...] properl[...] husband and wife kiss."

His voice sounded like leather against gravel.

She opened her mouth to suggest otherwise, but suddenly he bent his head and pressed his lips to hers.

He tasted of salt and the barest hint of whiskey. The kiss was pleasant, somewhat like the few she'd shared with Everett. Not too overpowering—nice, even.

A measure of confidence returned and she relaxed. Perhaps Rowe Mercer wasn't as frightening as she'd first thought. Without thinking, she eased against him, splaying her fingers against his chest.

At her slight encouragement, a deep moan rumbled in his chest. His kiss grew more insistent and he pushed his tongue between her lips. Raw desire radiated from him, and she knew instantly this kiss was nothing like Everett's well-mannered pecks.

She was in over her head…!

* * *

The Perfect Wife
Harlequin Historical #614—June 2002

Acclaim for Mary Burton's recent books

The Colorado Bride
"A heart-touching romance about love,
loss and the realities of family."
—*Romantic Times*

A Bride for McCain
"This is a delightful Western romp....
A great first book for this new author!"
—*Old Book Barn Gazette*

"Newcomer Mary Burton is a delightful surprise for
Western romance fans as her genial tale...
will fully beguile readers."
—*Affaire de Coeur*

MARY BURTON
THE PERFECT WIFE

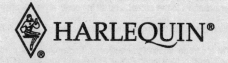

HARLEQUIN®

TORONTO • NEW YORK • LONDON
AMSTERDAM • PARIS • SYDNEY • HAMBURG
STOCKHOLM • ATHENS • TOKYO • MILAN • MADRID
PRAGUE • WARSAW • BUDAPEST • AUCKLAND

ISBN 0-373-29214-7

THE PERFECT WIFE

Copyright © 2002 by Mary Taylor Burton

Please address questions and book requests to:
Harlequin Reader Service
U.S.: 3010 Walden Ave., P.O. Box 1325, Buffalo, NY 14269
Canadian: P.O. Box 609, Fort Erie, Ont. L2A 5X3

To Betsy

Chapter One

September 1, 1876

Dear Mrs. Winslow,

I was happy to receive your second letter today. In answer to your questions, I live on a spread that's an hour's ride from Saddler Creek. The town has a mercantile, a schoolhouse and a hotel, but still is in need of women like you to smooth out its rough edges.

Mrs. Winslow, I prefer actions to words, so I'll get to my point. I liked what I read in your letters and believe we would be well suited in marriage. I will not woo you with promises of love, but I do offer my respect and a home where we can raise your daughter and, God willing, our sons. Together, we can build a fine life.

I await your reply.

Rowe Mercer

Jenna Winslow carefully folded Rowe Mercer's letter, praying again for a sign that she'd made the right decision to marry. She stared up into the gray, heavy sky, half expecting a crack of lightning, a sudden parting of the clouds, even a rainbow.

Of course, nothing happened.

Annoyed by her foolish need for reassurance, she tucked Mr. Mercer's letter between the pages of her crisp new copy of *Beeton's Book of Household Management,* then put both in her freshly oiled leather traveling valise by her feet. She smoothed kid-gloved hands over her forest-green skirt and for the third time adjusted the folds of her velvet cape.

"I don't need a sign. Everything's going to be fine," she whispered. "This move is best for both of us."

Jenna glanced into the white wicker basket sitting next to her on the railroad station bench, where her five-month-old niece, Kate, slept. The little girl's skin was as soft as down and her blond hair the color of snow. Her tiny lips curled into a pout.

Around them the Alexandria, Virginia, train station overflowed with gentlemen dressed in fine wool suits and black overcoats. Many escorted ladies in Worth dresses and capes trimmed with silk cording. All looked impatient as they huddled there, trying to stave off the morning's damp chill while waiting for the nine o'clock train, already twenty minutes late.

The brisk air, thick with moisture, promised an early winter. Jenna rubbed her cold hands together, sorry she wouldn't be here to see Alexandria's cobblestone streets and sleek town homes blanketed in snow one last time. She'd grown up in the city, and despite the hard times she'd endured here these last few months, many good memories made leaving more emotional than she'd imagined.

A whistle blew, signaling the approaching train, and prickling her nerves.

As she scanned the platform, Jenna glimpsed a man dressed in a gray suit staring boldly at her over the edge of his *Alexandria Gazette.* Raising her chin a notch, she held the man's gaze until he turned back to his paper.

The Winslow scandal had been the talk of Alexandria for months, and a day didn't pass without someone pointing or staring at her. She'd learned to live with her tarnished pedigree and not shrink behind her books. But there were still moments when she longed for the days when her sister was alive, and Jenna and her fiancé, Everett, had been so in love.

Kate stirred in her basket, opened her eyes and began to wail. Jenna picked her up and reached for a bottle tucked in the edge of the basket. Nestling the babe in the crook of her arm, she coaxed the nipple into her mouth and waited until she began to suckle the concoction of canned milk, water and molasses. As the baby relaxed and closed her eyes, the faint scent of milk wafted upward. Holding Kate bolstered Jenna's courage and reminded her of what was important.

The train's black, mud-splattered engine slowed as it came into the station and ground to a halt. Jenna's muscles throbbed with tension as black ashes fluttered from the smokestack and the air grew heavy with the smell of sulfur.

A conductor jumped down and placed a small set of wooden stairs in front of the passenger car.

An uncertain future taunted Jenna, and her worries roared to life. Fear told her to grab Kate and flee, even as she reminded herself that she'd run out of options.

She settled the baby back in her basket, tucked the blanket under her chin and rechecked her train ticket. Then she rose, proud that her knees wobbled only a little bit.

This was it.

"Jenna!" A tall, willowy man dressed in a brown suit and an elegantly tailored overcoat pushed his way through the busy station. His blond hair, normally neatly combed back, swept over blue eyes, which looked a little wild as he searched the crowd.

Relief fluttered through Jenna and her heart kicked. "Everett!"

Dr. Everett Patterson, the man she'd once promised to love forever, rushed toward her. "Jenna, thank God I found you in time."

A frosty breeze brushed her skirts. A part of her ached to reach out to him, to wrap her arms around him, but she didn't dare. "What are you doing here?"

Everett closed the distance between them in quick strides, then embraced her. "Don't go."

Hands fisted at her side, Jenna feared her resolve would shatter. "Everett, please."

"You didn't really think I'd let you get on this train, did you?"

"After our last argument—"

"I was wrong to be so hard on you." He gazed down at her, his eyes warming. "I've found a solution to our problem. I've spoken with Reverend Thompson. He's certain he can find a home for the baby."

Jenna drew back. "A home?"

He smoothed a blond curl from her forehead. "Yes. A family to adopt her. I don't know the particulars, but the reverend assures me that because the child is healthy and so young, she won't have to stay in the orphanage long. Two or three months at the most."

"But Everett—"

He cupped her face in his palms. "No need to thank me. I know what a terrible strain it's been, caring for the child. You must be so relieved."

"Relieved?" Even to her own ears Jenna's voice sounded brittle, angry. "Everett, have you forgotten that my parents spoke to Reverend Thompson right after Victoria's death? I refused to let them send Kate away then."

His hands slid to her slender shoulders. "But that was during a trying time. Your parents had just laid your sister to rest. You were upset, overtired. You needed something to cling to."

"I've told you a thousand times I'm not giving Kate up."

"I admire your courage, Jenna," he said with a touch of exasperation. "But enough is enough. That baby is not your problem."

Jenna flinched. "That baby's name is *Kate,* and my sister died giving birth to her. *Kate's* grandparents want nothing to do with her, and her father never bothered to claim her. I'm all *Kate* has. And I won't give her away.''

He jabbed long fingers through his fine hair. ''I thought you'd be more reasonable after I gave you time to think.''

''Time to think?'' She stiffened as if he'd slapped her.

''You didn't fully understand how cruel life can be, Jenna.''

''That's why you refused all my visits and notes these last few months?'' Unladylike fury whipped through her. ''You shut me out so I'd be driven to desperation.''

''I had to show you how much you need me. You're my plain, little bookworm. You understand literature, history and art. You've been wonderful with my patients, but you're not always in touch with the real world.''

''I've managed these last months without your help.''

He leaned closer, his voice low. ''Come on, Jenna. You're not doing so well. Your parents have left town and none of your friends will accept you in their homes. You're living in rented rooms and have sold most of your possessions.''

''I don't need *things.*''

''Really? Then why respond to that mail-order bride ad?''

She shrugged. "I explained in my note to you that it was the most logical course."

What Everett didn't know was that she'd posted her first letter more out of anger than conviction, believing Everett would be shocked out of his mood and come around. But he hadn't. And then Mr. Mercer had responded. And she'd replied, still hoping Everett would concede.

But he hadn't given an inch.

So she'd written back to Mr. Mercer, intent on doing what she must to keep Kate safe.

"I know you too well, Jenna. You answered that ad to make me mad. Well, if it will make you feel any better, it did. You had me tied in knots. And I honestly never thought you'd take your farce this far." He chuckled, as if humoring a child. "But enough is enough. It's time to stop playing games."

She stared at his refined features, which had once been so dear to her. He'd become a stranger. "I am getting on this train."

His smile vanished. "You'd never lower yourself to be a mail-order bride."

"Lots of women are mail-order brides," she said, grateful her voice sounded so calm.

"Not women like you. You're society bred, educated."

"What good is education and breeding when

you don't have a nickel to your name or anyone to rely on?''

He straightened his shoulders. ''You have me.''

''With conditions.''

His narrowing mouth emphasized his frustration. ''If you want unconditional love, Jenna, get a dog. And don't tell me that this man, who had to advertise to get a wife, doesn't have expectations.''

''He wants children.''

Everett clenched his fingers as if clinging to his composure. ''We were supposed to have our *own* children one day.''

For two years, she'd dreamed of having Everett's children. Letting go of that vision had been the harshest consequence of her decision to leave. ''I know,'' she said softly.

''We still can, if you'll only surrender this child.''

''No.''

He cursed and smacked his fist against his thigh. ''You are throwing away our dreams!''

She had desperately wanted things to be different. But they weren't. ''I won't abandon Kate.''

He snorted in disbelief. ''Don't tell me this man you're marrying doesn't care about the scandal.''

She raised a delicate eyebrow. ''Not all men are so concerned about what others think!''

The businessman had lowered his paper a fraction and cocked an ear, taking in their every word. Two finely dressed women had stopped talking, and stole glances at them.

Everett cursed and lowered his voice. "You don't love *him*."

The morning cold had seeped into Jenna's bones, making her restless. "Love is a poor second to security—a lesson I learned well these last few months."

He muttered an oath. "You're not cut out for frontier life, Jenna. You're accustomed to the finer things. You'll wither and die in that godforsaken land."

"I will be fine."

Everett shifted his weight and shoved his hands in his pockets. "You don't know how to cook."

"I will learn."

"You've never seen a laundry tub. You'll be a failure as a rancher's wife."

Color rose in Jenna's cheeks. "I think I've heard enough from you."

The conductor approached her, touched the bill of his cap. "Ma'am, you need help with your luggage?"

Jenna pulled free of Everett's grip. "Yes. I also have several crates that the ticket master is holding."

The conductor peered over his glasses. "I'll take care of it. May I see your ticket?"

"Of course." Her hand trembled as she pulled the ticket out of her valise and handed it to him. Kate started to cry.

The conductor nodded. "Saddler Creek, Colorado. That's mighty far from here. Not much of a town. What takes you out there?"

She hesitated, unable to look at Everett as the words tumbled from her lips. "I'm meeting my husband-to-be."

The conductor nodded with approval as he stamped the ticket. "I'll say one thing about your intended, he's taking good care of you."

Jenna lifted Kate out of her basket and hugged her close. The baby grew quiet, her little fingers fisted around Jenna's finger. "I don't understand."

"First-class seats for you and the baby. It's a real luxury to have the extra room for such a long trip. The train's booked solid." He handed the ticket back to her and picked up Kate's basket. "I'll put this in your seat. Enjoy your trip."

"Thank you."

Only after the conductor had left did she face Everett. "I have to leave now."

"You're *not* being reasonable. In time—"

"I've run out of time!"

Her sharp, loud tone startled the baby, who

started to fuss again. Jenna jostled the child, trying to calm her, but her own knees felt weak, her body drained by anger and fear. She was so tired of fighting.

Everett ground his teeth. "You don't understand the position you've put me in. My practice has suffered since all this mess started."

"That's not my fault."

"This whole situation is Victoria's fault. It was always like your sister to muck things up. Only Victoria could manage to get with child mere months before her marriage to another man."

Jenna flinched. "It takes two people to make a baby."

"Men can be forgiven for their indiscretions, but women are held to a higher standard, Jenna."

Jenna's parents had agreed with Everett on that point. When they'd discovered Victoria was pregnant, they'd beaten her, demanding she reveal the name of the baby's father. When she'd refused, they'd exiled her to the country, hoping she'd deliver in secret. They'd told everyone that she'd gone to New York to shop for accessories for her trousseau, hoping they could salvage their prized reputation and Victoria's impending wedding. But Victoria had died unexpectedly in childbirth, leaving the family with a squalling infant no one except Jenna had wanted.

James and Doris Winslow had left town two days after their young daughter's funeral. They claimed grief had driven them away. Jenna knew it was shame.

Her heart tightened a notch as she looked down into the child's eyes, wide-open now and focused on her. She watched the rapid rise and fall of the babe's chest and noted how her lips pouted. She was so trusting. "None of that matters now."

He glared at the child. "If she'd only died with Victoria, everything would have been fine."

Jenna stepped back. "I've heard enough."

As she turned to leave, he followed, hovered close, his lips next to her ear. "Victoria had many lovers. Any one of them could be the child's father."

Jenna froze. Caution had become a well-honed reflex since Kate's birth. "That was a lie spread by the gossips."

"It's no lie. Victoria was not the innocent she portrayed herself to be. Your parents thought they kept a tight rein on her, but she was very clever and slipped out often."

For a moment Jenna couldn't breathe. "You're wrong."

"I wish I were," he said miserably.

There was something about him—a shift in energy, an aura of guilt. A stark realization struck

Jenna. She didn't know how she knew, but she did. "You were with her."

He nodded his downcast head. "Yes." The pure anguish in his voice attested to his honesty. "And I'll curse the day she lured me into her bed."

Jenna had thought there was nothing else Everett could do to hurt her, but she'd been wrong. For an instant she nearly crumbled. Instead, she shoved the pain deep inside her and locked it away, knowing she would deal with it later. "How could you?"

"It was one foolish, drunken moment." He flexed his tense fingers. "I wasn't Victoria's first, and she was quite willing."

Unshed tears burned the back of Jenna's throat. "Are you Kate's father?"

"No. Maybe. I don't know." His fingers bit into her arm. "Please, Jenna, you have to understand I have a reputation to protect. If the child grew up to resemble me, it would ruin me. My medical practice, my patients—they wouldn't tolerate such an indiscretion. You must understand now why the child can't stay in Alexandria."

"I understand," she said.

His shoulders slumped with relief. "Then you can forgive me. We can go back to the way things were." When he hugged her close, he didn't seem to notice how rigid she stood. "I've missed having you with me, helping me with my patients."

"Goodbye, Everett."

Confusion flickered across Everett's face. "But I thought—"

She jerked away from his embrace. "You thought wrong."

Rage hardened his soft features. "You're a fool. You would have wanted for nothing if you'd married me."

"Except dignity, respect."

"Both will be poor consolation when you're scraping to get by on some godforsaken ranch."

The conductor cupped his hand around his mouth and shouted, "All aboard!"

She turned away from Everett, walked to the train and climbed the four narrow steps. Her feet felt as if they were made of lead, and it took every ounce of her courage to board the train.

Tears pooling in her eyes, she struggled with her skirts and Kate as she made her way down the crowded aisle. Passengers were packed in sometimes three to a seat, and the air was heavy with the smells of old cigar smoke and stale food. A farmer with his feet propped up on the armrest in front of him stared at her as she passed. A woman dressed in black sat with her four runny-nosed children.

Grateful to pass through the car, Jenna moved into the connecting first-class compartment. This car had as much space as the other, but half the number of passengers. The air was lighter, the carpet thick, and the windows were draped in a rich fabric. She quickly found her seat in the back, and Kate's basket, which the conductor had placed on the empty seat next to hers.

Relieved, Jenna laid Kate down in her basket. The child yawned, stretched her arms and gurgled, unaffected by the massive changes in their lives.

Jenna collapsed into her seat, surprised it was so plush and comfortable. She turned to the window. Everett stood on the platform, his chin thrust in the air. He met her gaze one last time, then turned and strode into the sea of people.

Her emotions in shambles, Jenna settled back in her seat, her hand resting possessively on Kate's basket. Noisy chatter filled the car. Two seats down sat a young couple, their heads only inches apart as they talked in excited whispers. Another woman, five seats in front of Jenna, laughed with her two young children. Across the aisle two men discussed the price of beef.

Amidst all the noise and activity, Jenna felt completely alone. Her uncertain future loomed large. Kate's upbringing now rested solely on her shoulders, and the responsibility weighed heavily.

She touched the child on the cheek and managed a smile. "I love you, Katie-bug. No matter what he said, you are my child now and nothing will ever change that."

Kate blew a spit bubble and smiled.

Jenna reached into her valise and pulled out Rowe Mercer's letter. As she stared at his bold script, the what-ifs stalked her like a pack of hungry wolves.

Dear Mrs. Winslow.

Despite her brave words to Everett, she didn't know much about Rowe Mercer, and she hadn't been completely honest with him.

She nibbled her bottom lip. She'd been candid on most points and had stretched the truth only once. Or twice.

Dear Mrs. Winslow.

She stared out the window, watching the warehouses and stores slowly turn to homes, then shanties and finally rolling grasslands.

She folded the letter neatly and tucked it back in her reticule, willing her nerves to calm as she focused on the rhythmic rocking of the train car.

Dear Mrs. Winslow.

The truth was she'd flat-out lied to Mr. Mercer. She had told him she was a widow with her own young child to raise. She'd feared he'd reject her outright if he knew why she needed to marry.

Now she prayed that, once they met face-to-face and she explained her true circumstances, he would understand.

Charlie Bingham, Saddler Creek's telegraph officer, peered over the wire rim of his glasses at Rowe Mercer. Mercer's broad shoulders and tall frame dominated the tiny office.

Charlie had always been treated fairly by Mr. Mercer during the seven years he'd known him, but the powerfully built rancher scared the living daylights out of him.

Mercer had worked hard, built a wealthy ranch and lived a peaceable life since he'd moved to Saddler Creek, but his gray eyes bore into folks when he spoke and made them feel as if they were in the crosshairs of a rifle. The ragged scar that ran past his left eye to the corner of his mouth reminded everyone of his violent, bounty-hunting past. Some said he'd killed a dozen men, others said it was close to a hundred. No one knew for certain and no one had dared to ask.

"Need a telegram sent today?" Charlie said, proud that his voice didn't waver.

Rowe scrawled out a note and handed it to him. "That's right."

His shoulder-length, dark hair accentuated his strong jaw, which was covered in dark stubble. His muddy range coat hung open, revealing denim pants that hugged his muscular legs and lean waist.

Charlie offered a wan smile and glanced down at the note, reading it quickly. "You're sending a telegram to the judge?"

"That's right."

Charlie's curiosity overcame his fears. Rowe Mercer wasn't a man to call upon the law unless there was real trouble. "Mind my asking why you need a judge?"

"For a wedding."

"Who's getting married?"

"Me."

Charlie rocked back on his feet. "To who?" The handful of marriageable women who lived within fifty miles had been warned by their mamas to stay clear of Rowe Mercer. "I mean, if you don't mind me asking."

Rowe studied him a beat longer, then shrugged. "Jenna Winslow."

"She ain't from around here."

"Virginia."

"Planning a big wedding?"

"Nope." Rowe pulled out two bits and handed them to Charlie. "See that the telegram gets sent right away. I want the judge here by Friday."

"Yes, sir."

Without a word, Rowe stalked out of the telegraph office, his spurs jangling.

From his barred telegraph window, Charlie watched the rancher stride down the street. Folks naturally cleared a path when he passed. A few stopped to whisper to each other as he untied his reins and mounted his horse.

Charlie glanced down at the note. "I wonder if Jenna Winslow knows what she's getting herself into?"

Chapter Two

"Rowe Mercer, if I didn't know better, I'd swear you was nervous." The good-natured jab came from Pappy Davis, Rowe's foreman and close friend since Rowe's first cattle drive seven years ago.

Rowe glared down at the man, who stood only inches above five feet and sported a thick, bristly gray beard. "I'm irritated."

Truth was Rowe couldn't remember a time in recent years when he'd been as tense, but he wasn't about to admit it, even to Pappy.

Pappy's brown eyes danced with laughter. "I've known you too long, boy. When you look like you want to put your fist into a wall, you're nervous."

Rowe leaned against the weathered wall outside the saloon. He ignored the lively piano music and the smoke drifting out from the barroom, and forced his muscles to relax. "Don't you have anything else to worry about, old man?"

Pappy chuckled, unafraid of Rowe's fierce expression. "The stagecoach has been late before," he teased.

"Yep."

"And you sure ain't the first man to ever marry."

Rowe flexed his gloved fingers. "Nope."

"She'll get here sooner or later."

"Yep."

Rowe glared down the dusty main street of Saddler Creek, and its odd collection of buildings made mostly of freshly milled wood. No longer a sleepy town dependent on a half-dozen ranchers, the community was growing. The price of cattle was high, and many a man thinking to get rich quick had moved to Colorado to set up a homestead. In the last year alone, the town had added a hardware store, land title office, hotel and full-time smithy. The saloon and mercantile, the oldest establishments in town, now enjoyed a booming trade, and a schoolhouse would open in the spring.

Wagons rumbled down Main Street, past the newly built boardwalk filled with cowhands and a half-dozen women dressed in calico. The growing number of women were taming Saddler Creek and turning the once wild cattle town into a good place for a man to raise a family.

Rowe frowned at the thought, glaring through the double doors of the smoke-filled saloon at Judge Cyrus Tompkins, whom he'd brought in special for the wedding. The judge sat at a table with three cowhands, a tumbler brimming with hooch next to his stack of red and blue poker chips.

Pappy's gaze trailed Rowe's to the judge. "He can still hold his cards, so I reckon you've got an hour or two before he passes out."

Rowe wished there'd been a minister in town who could have performed the ceremony. Women seemed to like that kind of formality. "His nose is as red as a strawberry."

Judge Tompkins smacked his hand on the poker table and ordered another bottle.

Rowe ground his teeth. Waiting was never his strong suit, and he felt as if he might jump out of his skin. "If the stage doesn't get here with my bride before Tompkins passes out, I'll have to spend the night in town. I don't want to lose another morning's work."

"You've lost days before," Pappy said. "You're just vexed because you're not in the driver's seat for once."

Pappy was right, partly. But what rankled Rowe more than waiting was this restless, uneasy feeling in the pit of his stomach—a feeling that had been with him since the day he'd asked Jenna Winslow to be his wife. It wasn't like him to feel so off center. He'd handled renegades, droughts and blizzards better than ordering a bride.

Pappy clapped his gnarled hand on Rowe's rock-hard shoulder. "Relax. You're tighter than a tangled rope wrapped around a calf stuck in a mud hole."

Rowe allowed a small grin. "Once I'm married, I'll get back into my old routine and everything will be fine."

Pappy scratched his beard. "A wife has a way of changing things. They ain't always as accommodating as a man would like."

"Mine will be."

Pappy chuckled. "You think?"

"Absolutely. Jenna Winslow understands our marriage is an arrangement of sorts. She and her child get a good home and I get sons."

"Well, as long as you are clear about your plans, I suppose your wife will be right manageable," Pappy teased.

Wife. The word hadn't ever been linked with Rowe Mercer's name, and it sounded strange to his ears. He'd never given much thought to having a wife until last spring, when he'd been riding his property.

The Crossfire Ranch stretched for fifty miles. Filled with pride that April day, he'd looked out over the rolling hills, then down at the homestead, remembering how he'd built every inch of that place with his own hands, overcoming weather and rustlers, and sometimes spilling his own blood to make the land his.

But as the blustering wind had whipped over the hills, he'd been struck by a deep sense of loneliness. Despite all his hard work, there was no one to share his successes with. Sure, there was Pappy, and other hired hands who were loyal and honest, but there were no children to teach riding and roping to, or to fill the fancy house he was building. Suddenly, it didn't seem right that a man nearing his thirty-sixth birthday didn't have children.

Then and there, he'd decided he would advertise for a wife to give him sons.

Of course, he couldn't start making those generations until his bride arrived. Rowe reached in his pocket and pulled out a gold watch he'd bought secondhand in Denver last month. The watch was finely crafted, but more important, he liked its worn look, as if it had been passed down from father to son. He imagined his son having that watch, keeping it safe.

Twelve past two. The stage was four hours late. When was she going to arrive?

He snapped the watch closed and peered inside the saloon. "That damn judge isn't gonna make it if we don't get some coffee in him."

Pappy shrugged. "I reckon a little coffee wouldn't hurt."

"You're right." Rowe shoved the watch in his vest pocket, headed into the saloon and marched toward the judge's table. The floor was sticky with booze.

As Judge Tompkins lifted a full glass to his lips, Rowe plucked it out of his hand. "That's enough for today, Judge. I want you sober when my bride arrives."

Judge Tompkins looked up at Rowe with blood-shot eyes. He'd removed the stays from his starched collar and had unbuttoned his jacket, allowing his ample belly to spill over his belt. "Oh, come on, since when did you ever begrudge a man a drink or two?"

"One or two isn't the problem. Ten or twelve is."

"I can marry you with my eyes closed." He tapped a beefy finger against his temple. "I got all the marriage vows right up here, safe and sound."

Rowe hauled the judge to his feet. "If you're passed out, it doesn't really matter what's in your head. Let's go outside for some fresh air."

The judge pouted. "But Mr. Mercer, I'm winning."

"Quit while you're ahead," Rowe warned.

The grizzled cowhand who sat to Judge Tompkins's right studied Rowe with sharp eyes. "Mister, the judge said he wanted to stay, and I've a mind to win back some of the money he's won from me."

Rowe pinned the man with his gaze. "Some other time." He slid his hand to his holster.

The cowhand glanced at the rumpled bills scattered in front of the judge, then at Rowe's hand, as if weighing the merits of fighting. A tense moment passed before he pushed himself to his feet and glanced around at the men who were watching. "I ain't up to killing Mercer today," he growled.

"Likely you'd have been the one to die," Pappy said.

The cowhand grumbled a response, then strode out of the saloon.

The judge hiccuped as Rowe led him outside. "Rowe, what is it about you that scares the tar out of folks?"

"Can't say."

Rowe didn't dwell on the subject, because just then the stage rolled into town. Covered with mud, the rig looked to be in good shape except for a few missing spokes on the back wheel. Cullum Belford, a sandy-haired Scotsman, sat in the driver's seat, as he had for the last five years. The man looked tired and heaved a deep sigh as he pulled the team to a stop.

"Looks like your fiancée has arrived," Pappy said from behind the swaying judge.

"Yep." A familiar knot settled in the pit of Rowe's gut. "Take care of Tompkins, Pappy."

"And miss meeting your bride? No way. We're coming with you."

Rowe glowered at his friend, but didn't argue. Instead, he strode toward the wagon. His spurs jangled softly and his range coat flapped in the breeze as his long legs ate up the distance.

When he reached the coach, he rubbed his hand over his chin, which was covered in dark stubble. Suddenly he wished he'd taken the time to visit the barber while he'd been cooling his heels. Even under the best circumstances, he wasn't much to look at.

He pulled off his worn leather gloves and sighed. Like it or not, there wasn't much to be done about his appearance now. His bride-to-be would just have to get used to his looks.

Pappy joined Rowe, with the judge in tow. He propped Tompkins against the side of the stage and called a greeting to the stagecoach driver.

Cullum waved at Rowe and Pappy. "Didn't think we'd make it."

Mercer shook the man's hand. "Beginning to wonder that myself."

"Lost a wheel near Singingwoods. Took the better part of the morning to fix it."

"No other trouble?"

"Smooth as silk, my friend."

"Good."

Rowe wouldn't have minded if Cullum had had other troubles to hash out. Discussing everyday events soothed his nerves. But with nothing more to be said, he turned his attention to the door. As he reached for the handle, a woman wearing a blue bonnet stuck her head out of the window.

Her gaze locked on his for a handful of seconds before she looked past him, searching the crowd.

She was about the prettiest little thing he'd ever seen. Sunlight caught her pale hair, making him wonder if it was made of spun gold. Her skin was the texture of porcelain, and her delicately rounded lips the perfect shade of pink. Her blue eyes were the color of a clear winter sky.

Rowe heard Pappy's sharp intake of breath. Or was it his own?

Pappy jabbed him in the ribs. "She can't be yours. She's too pretty."

A wave of disappointment washed over Rowe.

Then, just as quickly, he shoved aside the emotion. Of course she was his. Women rarely came to Saddler Creek.

Rowe touched the brim of his hat. "Mrs. Winslow?"

She stopped her searching and swung her gaze back to his. Fear flickered in her sapphire eyes and she shrank back slightly. "Yes," she said with a slight hitch in her voice.

Damn, but she looked so young and fragile. He could hardly believe she was a widow with a young one of her own. Her youth reminded him again that he had passed his thirty-fifth year.

"I'm Rowe Mercer."

Her skin paled and her lips formed an O as she nodded.

Rowe wondered for a moment if he should have chosen the woman from Missouri—the one with three sons and a dozen years of farm experience— then rejected the notion. He liked the look of Jenna Winslow. He liked it a lot.

Pappy nudged him forward. "Don't let him scare you none, ma'am. I know Rowe ain't much to look at, but he cleans up pretty well."

Worry lines formed on her forehead, marring the flawless skin. "I see."

"That's enough out of you, Pappy." Rowe reached for the door handle and she drew back.

He jerked open the door as she pressed back against the coach seat and turned to fuss over a basket. A baby squawked. She picked up the basket, struggling to lift it in the confined space.

Instinctively, Rowe reached forward. "Let me help you, ma'am." Their gazes locked, and for an instant she wavered. Instead of being offended, Rowe admired her caution. A good mother watched over her younguns, and he wanted a good mother for his sons. "I'll be careful," he promised.

She studied him a beat longer, then handed the basket to him. "Thank you." Her voice sounded soft, cultured and clear.

He took the hamper and peeked inside at the baby, who was wrapped in a pink quilt. The babe was chewing on her fist, looking up at him fearlessly, with enormous eyes as bright and blue as her ma's. A fierce protectiveness washed over him. She wasn't his, but he knew he'd do right by her. "I suppose I'd best get used to toting young ones around. I want us to fill our house with children."

Mrs. Winslow blushed. "Yes."

The baby gurgled and Pappy peered in the basket. "The babe's a girl?"

"Her name is Kate," Mrs. Winslow said with pride.

Pappy nodded his bushy head. "Good thing.

Nothing sadder than a pretty boy. They get beat up a lot.''

Mrs. Winslow smiled. The worry lines wrinkling her brow eased. ''Thank you, I think, Mr., er…?

''No mister attached to my name. Folks call me Pappy.''

''Pappy,'' she repeated.

Holding the baby's basket in one hand, Rowe held out his other to Mrs. Winslow. She hesitated a second before she accepted it, her grip firm.

Mrs. Winslow stumbled on her long black cape as she climbed out of the coach, and had to lean on his shoulder to steady herself. He wrapped his arm around her narrow waist and easily lifted her down. She was as light as a feather, so he was surprised to note the fullness of her breasts as he lowered her to the dusty road.

''I reckon a strong winter gust would blow you right over,'' he said, his voice sounding rougher than he liked.

''I'm tougher than I look.''

She was nervous. He could tell by the flush of color in her cheeks and the way she nibbled her bottom lip. But she was doing her best to hide her fear. She had grit.

The judge tipped his hat and pushed away from the coach, the stench of whiskey strong. ''I'm Judge Cyrus Tompkins,'' he proclaimed in a slurred voice. "I've the pleasure of marrying you and Mr. Mercer today."

"Today?" she said. She raised her chin, her stance stiffening a bit. "I thought we might take a few days to get to know one another before we exchanged our vows."

Rowe captured her elbow in his hand. "With so many chores on the ranch, I don't have time to waste. Besides, the sooner we get on with the ceremony the sooner things will get back to normal."

She glanced at the baby's basket, and the worry line returned to her forehead. He feared she'd bolt and was relieved to hear her say, "All right."

Rowe nodded toward the hotel. "I suppose the lobby is as good as anyplace. Pappy, help the judge across the street."

"Sure, Boss."

With the baby basket in one hand and his bride-to-be's elbow in the other, Rowe strode across the dusty street toward the hotel. Mrs. Winslow's skirts rustled loudly as she hurried to keep pace with his long strides. He made a point to slow down.

He'd never been one to put stock in what other people thought, but he noted the way folks—especially men—stopped to stare at Mrs. Winslow. Likely, she was the most cultured woman to ever live in Saddler Creek—a real fish out of water. She walked with her shoulders back and her chin out—not snobbish or mean-spirited, but with an air reserved for folks brought up with money.

Rowe had to admit he was proud to have Jenna Winslow on his arm.

Anxious to marry, he wasn't inclined to start any conversations with his neighbors. The baby started to fuss a bit, and the judge looked green around the gills, but as luck would have it, no one stopped them, and they reached the hotel in two shakes.

The hotel wasn't fancy, but it was clean and had a reputation for good food. It sported polished wood floors and a classy round settee in the center of the lobby.

The clerk was Fred Avery, a man with thinning hair and ruddy cheeks. Holed up behind the front desk, Mr. Avery was surrounded by a dozen men and women clamoring for a room or an answer to a question. But when he saw Rowe enter, he moved to assist him.

Rowe shook his head. "Don't worry over me, Mr. Avery. Just going to borrow a corner of the lobby for a quick wedding ceremony."

The clerk raised his eyebrow in mild surprise. "Who's getting married?"

"Me."

Mr. Avery's mouth dropped open and the crowd in the lobby went silent. Men and women alike stared curiously at Mrs. Winslow, at Rowe, and then at Mrs. Winslow again. Several women shook their heads and one man grumbled something about rich folks being able to buy most anything.

Mr. Avery peered over the rim of his glasses, barely hiding his surprise. "Okay, Mr. Mercer."

Rowe set the basket down in a quiet corner on a rose-colored settee and shrugged off his coat as he looked at Mrs. Winslow. "Pappy's packed us a fine lunch. We'll eat it on the way to the ranch."

"We're not staying in town tonight?" Again, she had that panicked look.

Rowe wanted her not to worry, but he wasn't a man for pretty words or tact. "Too much work at the ranch."

The baby fussed louder and Mrs. Winslow picked up her daughter. The child, getting the attention she wanted, stopped her cries.

Mrs. Winslow took extra time to adjust Kate's small hand-knit jacket, as if turning over fresh worries. She didn't speak right away, but then, to his relief, she nodded. "Okay."

She kissed the baby on the forehead, then laid her down again in her basket. She graced the infant with a smile that tugged at Rowe's heart. The baby grinned.

Cooing to the child, she removed her hat, then undid the gold clasp of her cape, slipped it off and draped it on a chair next to her hat. She picked up the baby again.

Rowe drew in a measured breath as he stared from her full breasts to the narrow cut of her waist and hips. Her green traveling dress hugged her curves in just the right places. It had been a long time since a woman had stirred his blood like this.

"Judge, let's get down to business," Rowe said gruffly.

The judge hiccuped and pulled a small, worn Bible from his pocket. "Dearly beloved..."

The people in the lobby kept their distance, but remained silent. They'd formed a semicircle and stared openly.

The judge stifled a burp. "Sorry."

Mrs. Winslow stood close to Rowe but was careful not to touch him. Her head barely reached his shoulders, and the faint scent of rose water drifted up to him.

Rowe felt a tightening in his gut and itched to have the marriage done. "Okay, Judge."

The judge swayed back and forth, with one eye open and one closed, as if he were trying to focus. "We are gathered here today to join this man and woman in matrimony." He paused. "Does anyone have anything to drink? My throat's a bit dry."

Mrs. Winslow jostled the baby on her hip.

"Kate could use some canned milk. She'll be getting hungry any minute now."

Rowe flexed his fingers. "Mr. Avery," he called out to the desk clerk. "Send someone over to the restaurant and get canned milk."

The clerk, who was also staring at them, straightened. "Sure thing, Mr. Mercer."

The judge coughed. "I was thinking of something a bit stronger than milk."

"You can wait," Rowe said.

"But the baby gets her milk," he whined.

"Finish the ceremony," Rowe warned.

"Do you, Mrs...." Judge Tompkins paused, then frowned as he stared at Mrs. Winslow. "Madam, I seem to have forgotten your name."

"Genevieve Alexandra Winslow."

The judge blinked. "Yes, that's it. Do you, Genevieve Alexandra Winslow, take Rowe Mercer to be your husband?"

"Yes," she said finally.

Rowe released the breath he was holding, not quite believing he was about to have a wife.

"Do you, Rowe Mercer, take, uh...her to be your wife?"

"I do."

"Then by the powers given me by the state of Colorado, I now pronounce you man and wife. You can kiss the bride."

Rowe faced Jenna, not wholly comfortable kissing her with a roomful of people gawking.

His wife looked up at him, wide-eyed and worried, as if she was a virgin fresh from the schoolroom, which, of course, she wasn't. She was a widow woman with a babe on her hip to prove she knew the goings-on in a marital bed. He wanted to touch her, and cursed their lack of privacy. He itched to get home.

The judge cleared his throat. "Can I get a drink now?"

Rowe nodded, searching for a private spot where he could kiss his wife proper. "Tell Barney at the saloon that I'll pick up your tab for the evening."

The judge smiled, revealing yellowed teeth. "Much obliged, Mr. Mercer." He touched the brim of his hat. "Mrs. Mercer."

Rowe didn't pay much more mind to the judge, who hurried out of the hotel. Rowe felt good, as if he'd just finished a cattle drive and had gotten top dollar for his herd.

"Mrs. Mercer, let's get ourselves home. I believe if we get started this evening, we'll have a baby by summer."

Chapter Three

*S*ummer!

Jenna grew still. She'd just assumed there'd be some time—time to get acquainted with her new husband—before they shared a bed.

A wave of panic washed over her. She met Rowe's piercing gaze. Mr. Mercer had the eyes of a hunter, sharp and direct, absorbing every detail about her.

She'd been off balance from the moment they'd met. His expression, an odd mixture of surprise and naked longing, had set her senses on alert.

Now it was too late to run. Like it or not, she was married to this stranger.

"Are you ready to go home, Mrs. Mercer?" he said with a note of pride.

Mrs. Mercer. Her new name sounded so strange and final. She was aware then of the crowd that stared brazenly at them, a mixture of shock and amusement on their faces.

"I, uh…yes."

"You look a little pale."

"I'm just overwhelmed. This is all happening so fast."

"I don't waste time. If a job needs to be done, I do it."

Jenna felt her knees weaken, and was certain they'd have buckled if Rowe Mercer hadn't taken her arm.

He wasn't a handsome man, but he embodied a dauntless energy that frightened and excited her. He was nothing like the men she'd known, and instinct told her that he lived by his own code. He played by his own rules.

"I've got the milk," Mr. Avery called out.

Relieved for the reprieve, Jenna forced herself to give the clerk a bright smile. "Thank you."

Mr. Avery ducked his head and blushed. "Weren't no trouble at all. When I told my wife it was for the baby, she went ahead and mixed molasses and water in it. That's all right, ain't it?"

"It's perfect," Jenna said.

"I'll just set it on the table over here."

"Thank you again, Mr. Avery."

Mr. Avery brushed a greasy strand of hair back

over the bald spot on his head. "You two needing a room for the night?"

Mr. Mercer shook his head. "No. We'll be getting back to the ranch." He glanced at the townsfolk, who continued to gawk at Jenna, and then frowned. "I've too much work to spare the time."

Not knowing her husband, and overcome with her own worries, Jenna could only nod.

"Well, if you change your mind, you know you're always welcome," Mr. Avery said. "We always keep room six ready for you, Mr. Mercer." The clerk paused and looked at her with soulful eyes, as if he wanted to say something else. Instead, he returned to the front desk.

Kate started to fuss.

"If you will excuse me? The baby is hungry," Jenna said.

Mr. Mercer released her, allowing her to hurry to her reticule, which lay on the settee next to her cape. Focusing on the baby, she pulled out a bottle and unwrapped the clean cloth wound around it. Balancing the baby on her lap, she poured the milk mixture into the narrow opening and fastened on the nipple. The baby started to fuss louder, knowing what she was about to receive.

"She's got a fine set of lungs," Pappy said with a laugh. He hovered close.

"Yes," Jenna said. "She's got an appetite to match."

Mr. Mercer strode toward them. She didn't need to look up to know he was looming by her side, taking in every detail. Her hands trembled a bit as she stuck the nipple into Kate's mouth.

Pappy sat down on the settee next to Jenna. "Mind if I take a turn at feeding the little one? It's been awhile, but I reckon I could manage." He held up two clean hands. "Even washed my hands."

Pappy's old brown eyes possessed a hopefulness that she couldn't resist. She removed the bottle from Kate's mouth and carefully handed the baby over to him. Kate cried, frustrated that her meal had been interrupted, but Pappy remained unruffled and settled the child in the crook of his arm. He started to talk to Kate and she relaxed, allowing him to coax the nipple into her mouth. She latched on immediately and melted in Pappy's arms.

The knots binding Jenna's muscles loosened. "You've a way with babies."

Without taking his eyes off Kate, Pappy shrugged. "Rowe's put me in charge of the calves and whatever stray puppy finds its way to the ranch. I got a knack with little critters."

Jenna leaned closer. "Pappy, human infants are not like calves or puppies."

"You sure? I got a good bone in my saddlebag she can gnaw on."

Jenna sucked in a sharp breath. "A bone! Pappy, you can't give an infant a bone."

Mr. Mercer laid his hand casually on her shoulder. She started at the unexpected contact, sensed the restrained power in his long fingers. She glanced up at him. He took off his hat and tossed in on the settee. It landed on her cape.

His thick mane of black hair hung over his collar, and his eyes sparkled with laughter, making him look less fierce, more approachable. "He's pulling your leg."

"Oh."

Pappy grinned. "Mrs. Mercer, Baby Kate is fine. I've taken care of my share of human critters and I'd never let nothing happen to her. Get up, stretch your legs, have a word with that new husband of yours."

Her stomach rolled. "But—"

Mr. Mercer manacled her wrist with his long fingers. His touch was gentle, but unbreakable. "Stop worrying."

He tugged Jenna to her feet and guided her toward an alcove. When he noted the whispers and stares of the people in the lobby, he looked as if he'd speak. Frowning, he guided her the remaining paces to the small alcove, away from their prying eyes.

When they reached the dimly lit nook, all traces of humor had vanished from his eyes. He was looking at her as a starving man looked at a five-course meal.

Her stomach fluttered at the thought. The shadows slashed across his face, making the angles sharper. She forced herself to meet his gaze. "What can I do for you, Mr. Mercer?"

Slowly, he rubbed her jawbone with his callused thumb. "It's time you started calling me Rowe."

His touch made it hard for her to think. "Oh, I don't know. It's a bit informal. My mother never calls my father by his given name."

"This isn't the East, Jenna. We do things differently out here. Call me Rowe."

"Okay...Rowe." She started to leave. "If there's nothing else—"

He laid his hands on her shoulders, halting her retreat. "A marriage ceremony isn't properly finished until the husband and wife kiss." His voice sounded husky.

She opened her mouth to suggest otherwise, but before she could say a word, he bent his head and pressed his lips to hers.

He tasted of salt and the barest hint of whiskey. The kiss was pleasant, somewhat like the few she'd shared with Everett. Not too overpowering, nice even.

A measure of confidence returned and she relaxed. Perhaps Rowe Mercer wasn't as frightening as she'd first thought. Without thinking, she eased against him, splaying her fingers against his chest.

At her slight encouragement, a deep moan rumbled in his chest. His kiss grew more insistent and he pushed his tongue between her lips. Raw desire radiated from him, and she knew instantly that this kiss was nothing like Everett's well-mannered pecks.

Oh God, oh God, oh God.

She was in over her head.

The invasion set her senses reeling. Rowe continued to explore the soft depths of her mouth, and somewhere between confusion and fear, she started to enjoy the kiss.

Her fingers bunched in the worn cotton of his shirt as myriad emotions swirled through her. She wasn't sure what she feared more—him or the primitive, unfamiliar feelings stirring inside her.

Without warning, he pulled away. A dark smile curved the edges of his full mouth. He brushed a stray curl from her forehead as he stared down at her parted, moist lips.

His voice was a low, raspy growl. "We'd best get home."

A baby in the summer.

As the full import of his words sunk in, she had to fight to keep her voice steady. "How long does it take to get to your ranch?"

"An hour."

Her chest grew tight. "That's closer than I imagined."

His grip on her shoulders tightened a fraction. "There a problem?"

"No. Yes." She hesitated, feeling the color rise in her cheeks.

His eyes narrowed. "Speak your mind, Jenna."

As she stared at the buttons on his shirt, she'd have given anything if she could melt into the floorboards at this very moment and avoid discussing such personal matters. "I know you want a baby in the summer, and I'm happy to oblige." Her lips still tasted of him and her heart kicked against her chest. "But I need more than a few hours before we can, well, you know."

With his index finger, he pushed her chin up so her gaze met his. "What are you saying?"

Frustrated, she wondered why he didn't understand her meaning. "About tonight."

"Yes?"

She straightened her shoulders, wishing he wasn't staring so intently at her with his gray eyes. "I'd rather stay in a spare room."

He frowned. "Why?"

"I just need a little time to get to know you better."

"You're my wife."

"Yes, but we only just met. I mean, I know we've written several letters back and forth, but it would be nice if we could get acquainted before we—"

"Acquainted?" he said.

"You know, spend a little time together—maybe even talk."

"Talk?" His voice filled with disbelief. "We're married."

"We've a whole lifetime together," she said, frustrated. "Can't we just wait a little while before we—you know?"

"How much time do you need before you'll become a real wife?" His voice had grown gruff.

"Two months," she offered.

His frown deepened. "I'll give you two weeks."

"Six weeks," she bargained quickly, hardly believing she was negotiating her wedding night.

He shook his head. "One month and that's my final offer."

The hard set of his jaw told her he wasn't going to budge. "One month." She held out her hand to seal the bargain with a handshake.

He clasped his hand around hers. "Not a day longer, Jenna."

Her name sounded sensual when he spoke it. Goose bumps puckered the flesh on her arms. "I promise."

He nodded as if satisfied, then guided her back to the settee, where Pappy sat feeding Kate. The crowd remained in the lobby, and more people had gathered outside on the boardwalk by the window. They stood in shocked disbelief, whispering to each other.

Just then a woman burst through the main door of the hotel. She was large and wore a crisply starched blue cotton dress with a high collar trimmed with lace. She sported a derby-style hat cocked jauntily on her head, and carried a reticule embellished with glistening beads.

Her high button shoes clicked efficiently on the bare wooden floor as her hips swayed in time with her oversized bosom. "Mr. Mercer," she called out cheerfully. "I rushed right over here as soon as I heard."

Rowe's grip on Jenna's elbow tightened, indicating he'd heard the woman, but he didn't answer. He continued with Jenna toward Pappy and Kate.

The woman waved a delicate lace handkerchief. "Mr. Mercer," she said. Her voice was louder and firmer this time.

Rowe released a resigned sigh and turned. "Mrs. Brown."

The older woman's gaze bypassed Rowe and locked on Jenna. Her mouth dropped open.

Rowe shifted restlessly. "What do you want, Mrs. Brown?"

The woman recovered and straightened. Not taking her eyes off Jenna, she said, "We'd all heard you'd planned to marry, but I...we were expecting...I mean to say we weren't expecting your intended to be a lady."

Rowe tensed. "Mrs. Brown, this is my wife, Jenna. Now if you'll excuse us..."

Mrs. Brown ignored his dismissal. She thrust out a meaty, lace-gloved hand to Jenna. "My name is Evelyn Brown. My husband owns the mercantile and I am the chairwoman of the new school committee. We live in the big white clapboard house at the end of the street. I'm sure you saw it on your way into town."

Jenna shook her head, still stunned from her hasty vows and Rowe's kiss. "I'm sorry, I must have missed it. I was a bit distracted."

Mrs. Brown squeezed Jenna's hand. "Of course you were, dear. Here I'm expecting you to notice the local architecture and you're on your way to meet your husband." She cupped her fingers near her mouth and lowered her voice. "No one even knew he was thinking marriage until a couple of hours ago.''

Jenna glanced up at Rowe, wondering why he'd kept her arrival secret.

"So tell me," Mrs. Brown prattled on, "where are you from?"

"Mrs. Brown," Rowe interrupted. "There will be time for you and Jenna to talk later. Right now, I want to get her home."

As Rowe started to turn with Jenna, Kate squawked. Mrs. Brown's gaze shot past the two of them and locked on the infant. "A baby! I do love babies." She pushed past Jenna and Rowe and marched up to Pappy, who held the child protectively.

Mrs. Brown chucked Kate under the chin and cooed, "Well, aren't you a pretty little thing."

Kate's smile vanished and she thrust out her lower lip.

Pappy drew the child back. "You're scaring her."

"Nonsense, babies love me."

As Pappy grumbled something about busybodies, Mrs. Brown tickled the baby under the chin again. "Is she yours, Mrs. Mercer?" she asked over her shoulder.

For the first time since Kate's birth, Jenna didn't hesitate to reply. "Yes, she's mine."

"So you're a *widow*," she said, turning her full

attention back to Jenna. "You look so young, so slim. And to think you've already had a baby and buried a husband. How old are you anyway, my dear?"

Rowe stepped between Jenna and Mrs. Brown. "It's time my family and I get home."

"I don't see why you're in such a rush, Mr. Mercer," Mrs. Brown said. Annoyance had crept into her voice. "Surely Mrs. Mercer would like to stop by my house for tea. The stagecoach ride from the rail station is long and dusty."

"I'd love to," Jenna said as she took Kate from Pappy. She wasn't quite ready to be alone with her husband, and a cup of tea would go a long way to settling her nerves.

Rowe shook his head. "Some other time."

Jenna frowned, disappointed, but couldn't ignore years of her mother's training, which dictated no public disagreements. "Of course."

Mrs. Brown bristled, clearly not hampered by the same notion. "Your wife deserves a proper welcome, Mr. Mercer. Surely you understand she needs time to acquaint herself with her new neighbors."

Rowe tugged the brim of his hat lower. "Not today."

"You are a hopeless ruffian, Mr. Mercer." Disregarding his frown, Mrs. Brown shifted her attention to Jenna. "Don't worry, my dear, I shall see that you're properly welcomed to this town if it's the last thing I do."

"Thank you for your kindness," Jenna said.

The older woman touched Kate's foot and smiled. "If you need anything, do not hesitate to call on me."

"Again, thank you," Jenna said.

With Jenna and Kate at his side, Rowe started toward the door.

Pappy chuckled. "You've never had me or Rowe to tea before."

"Why would I have two uncultured cattlemen to tea?" She tugged the edge of her bodice down over her round belly.

Pappy waved the old woman away, but Rowe's body grew rigid for an instant. Jenna thought he might stop and say something more to Mrs. Brown, but he let go of whatever was on his mind and led her outside.

The sky was a crystal blue and the sun bright as they strode toward a wagon loaded with supplies, covered with a tarp and parked near the livery. Built for service, not style, the vehicle looked uncomfortable, and Jenna dreaded climbing onto the hard seat. Two days on a rickety stage and a week-long train ride had left her feeling bruised and exhausted. She dreaded the ride to come.

Sensing her hesitation, Rowe stopped short when they reached the wagon. "I reckon you're used to a lot of fancy teas and women like Mrs. Brown.''

Since the day she'd left the nursery, it was all Jenna had known. Working at Everett's clinic had been the only, much-welcomed reprieve from the stifling life. ''Yes.''

He rubbed his jaw as if searching for the right words. ''I know Saddler Creek isn't fancy like Alexandria. Mrs. Brown's the closest thing we have to what you were used to. I'd rather take a bullet than have tea with her, but I won't deny you your own kind. I can't say when we'll be back in town next, so if you want to stay an hour or two longer and visit with her you can.''

Jenna was touched. He didn't understand, but he was trying. ''I'd rather go home.''

He smiled. ''I'll hitch up the wagon.''

Laughter and excited voices drifted across the street from the hotel. The crowd on the boardwalk had grown threefold. Women dressed in calicos giggled, while the men jabbed each other in the ribs, as if sharing a bawdy joke or two. The easy camaraderie among the townsfolk reminded Jenna that she was an outsider with no community of her own. She wondered if the lonely, don't-quite-belong feeling that had plagued her for months would ever pass.

Pappy chortled as he came up behind her. ''I'll

be riding ahead now to see that supper's ready when you arrive.''

''You won't be riding with us?'' Jenna said.

''You don't need a salty old dog like me tagging along. The ride home will give you and Rowe a chance to get to know each other.''

''Of course,'' she whispered. The uncomfortable wagon seat didn't bother her so much now. Being alone with Rowe, even though he was her husband, did.

One month. A hard lump formed in her chest.

''Rowe Mercer, you sly dog!'' a friendly voice called from down the street. ''I ride into town to get supplies and the first bit of news I hear is that you got yourself hitched!''

Jenna looked past Rowe to see a tall, lanky man wearing faded overalls and a floppy brown hat. The man extended his hand to Rowe. Beside him stood a plainly dressed woman. Her build was sturdy and her brown hair, streaked with gold, was pinned back into a loose topknot. A basket filled with apples hung from the crook of her arm. Like the man beside her, her eyes sparkled with laughter.

Rowe's grim expression turned into a genuine smile as he accepted the man's hand and nodded to the woman. ''Sure did, Matt. Laura, I hope you're keeping this one out of trouble.''

''Every chance I get,'' she said with a laugh.

Jenna straightened and stepped forward so

Rowe's body no longer blocked her from the Holts' view. On reflex, she smoothed her skirts, wanting to make a good impression.

Rowe stood protectively beside her, pressing his hand to the small of her back. "Jenna, I'd like you to meet our neighbors, Matt and Laura Holt. Their ranch is an hour north of ours."

When Matt and Laura lowered their gazes to her, their grins vanished. Matt's mouth dropped open.

Jenna shifted the baby, then extended her gloved hand. "Pleased to meet you."

Laura recovered first. She wiped her hand on her skirt before accepting Jenna's. "Pleasure, Mrs. Mercer."

"Call me Jenna. This is Kate."

Laura's eyes softened as she looked at the baby. "Oh, she's lovely. Matt, isn't she beautiful?"

"Sure is," he said, still staring at Jenna as if in a daze.

"Matt and I have never been blessed with children, but we love them," Laura said. "I hope you both will come by for a visit before the winter sets in."

"I'd like that." Jenna glanced at Matt, wondering why he kept staring.

Laura jabbed Matt in the ribs. "Matthew Holt, you weren't raised in a barn. Stop staring as if you'd never seen a lady before. Show some manners."

Matt murmured something unintelligible and swung toward Rowe. "She is *your wife*."

"Yes, Matt." Rowe placed his hand on Jenna's shoulder. His long, well-formed fingers sent a shiver of awareness through her body.

Matt tipped his hat back on his head with his forefinger, still staring at Jenna as if he couldn't quite believe his eyes. "Sorry. It's just when you was talking about maybe one day taking a wife, I was expecting someone…sturdier."

Laura smiled brightly, hooked her arm around her husband's and jerked him close, as if she wanted to break his arm. "Maybe it's best if we say our goodbyes." She smiled warmly at Jenna. "We'll be looking forward to seeing you all soon."

Matt snapped out of his stupor. His cheeks turned crimson. "Yes, got to be going. A lot of work to do."

Rowe nodded and they exchanged hasty goodbyes.

As Matt and Laura hurried away, Matt leaned toward his wife, speaking louder than he must have realized. "She won't make it through the winter."

Chapter Four

Jenna sat ramrod straight next to her new husband on the front seat of his buckboard, cradling Kate in her arms as the wagon rumbled along the dusty road toward her new home. Each bump in the road jostled her against Rowe's hard, muscled thigh and reminded her of the dark, primitive kiss they'd shared at the hotel. As she stared at his strong hands clenching the reins, she couldn't shake the image of those hands touching her.

She was sorry Pappy had ridden ahead to the ranch and left them alone. The old man's lively banter would have helped ease her nerves.

The wagon wheel hit a rut and Jenna's leg again bumped Rowe's. As she had each time before, she drew away.

Rowe kept his eyes trained on the road ahead, but she noted his grip tightened on the reins. "You miss him?" His voice was tense.

Jenna started at the unexpected sound. He'd not spoken since they'd left town a half hour ago. "Who?"

"Your first husband."

She shifted uncomfortably. Lying didn't come easy for her. "I try not to think about him."

A wrinkle creased his forehead. She sensed the answer didn't satisfy him, and braced for another question.

Rowe cleared his throat. "We'll only talk about him this one time, but I want to know something about him."

She stared toward the rugged mountains. Her thoughts strayed to Everett, the man she'd loved— the man who would have been her husband if circumstances had been different. "His name was Everett," she said quietly. The lies didn't seem so awful if woven with the truth.

"How'd you meet?"

"At a party two years ago. He'd just returned from medical school up north, and he'd come to Alexandria to set up his practice."

"He was a doctor," Rowe said, more to himself than to her.

"Yes. On Thursdays, he operated a clinic in the church fellowship hall. I volunteered to help, and before long we became close."

The wagon wheels turned a dozen more times before he asked, "How'd he die?"

Unexpectedly, genuine tears pooled in her eyes. Everett was alive and well, but she mourned the love they'd shared. "I'd rather not talk about Everett." Her voice broke at what would likely be the last time she ever mentioned her former fiancé's name.

Rowe cleared his throat. "You loved him a lot."

"Yes."

He nodded, grim faced. "I reckon a part of you always will." A sharper edge had crept into his voice.

It vexed her that she still harbored feelings for Everett, even after he'd failed her so miserably. She prayed time would erase her lingering affection. "He was my past. You are my future."

Rowe turned and studied her face, the muscles in his jaw working. "Kate's bound to ask about him."

A bitter taste settled in her mouth. She never wanted Kate to know about Everett, a man who might or might not be her father. "He didn't want her."

Rowe scowled. "Why not?"

Surprised at her own candor, she said, "She didn't fit into his grand plans."

For several minutes Rowe was silent. Finally, he

said, "I'm the only pa Kate will ever know and I already consider her my own, so if you're willing, we won't tell her about *him*."

Jenna's throat constricted. "That means more to me than you'll ever know."

Without thinking, she laid her hand on his thigh. The touch was born of tenderness and gratitude, and at that moment it was as if they'd known each other a lifetime. Without glancing down, Rowe covered her hand with his and gave it a quick gentle squeeze.

Rowe had given her more support and help in a few hours than Everett had in six months. Her husband deserved to hear the truth from her, and Jenna was sorry she didn't have the courage to tell him everything. She withdrew her hand, more ashamed of herself than she'd thought possible.

They rode in silence for another mile or two before they reached the main entrance to Rowe's ranch. He pulled the wagon to a stop at a gate twelve feet high, fashioned out of logs. From the top hung a timber plank with Crossfire Ranch burned into it. The sign swayed softly in the breeze, squeaking as it moved.

Acres and acres of sun-cured grass spread as far as the eye could see. Tall, purple-gray mountains capped with snow stood far off in the distance.

Jenna shielded her eyes with her hand, drinking in the landscape. "It's beautiful."

"When I first laid eyes on this country, I thought the mountains were thunderclouds. They looked so much like the ones we'd see in Missouri, coming up the river before a storm."

"I don't think I could ever get tired of looking at them."

He sat a fraction taller. "I never have."

She stared out over the miles of rolling terrain. "How much land is yours?"

"I've two thousand five hundred acres or so."

"It's difficult to even imagine so much beauty."

"Don't be fooled by it. This is untamed, dangerous country."

Her gaze drifted across the endless miles. In the distance she spotted a small trail of smoke curling into the sky. "Is that your house?"

"Yes."

"How much farther?"

"A mile."

"That far?" Struck by the isolation, Jenna hugged Kate closer to her breast. "It's so unlike Alexandria. There the houses touch, crowded a dozen to a block."

"Never cared much for cities. Too much like cages."

She couldn't picture Rowe living happily in a

city. Like a wild animal, he needed land to roam. She'd never considered herself hemmed in by the city until today.

Rowe snapped the reins and goaded the horses forward. When they arrived at his ranch house, the sun was slipping behind the mountains, bathing the land in firelight.

Rowe's home was a one-story frame house with weathered siding in need of whitewashing, a steep roof, and a wide front porch cluttered with barrels and crates. There wasn't a blade of grass or a flower around the place. It looked more suitable for rough men than a young family.

To the right of the house stood a good-size log cabin made of hewn logs, which she guessed was the bunkhouse. To the left stood a barn, its doors wide-open. Inside stood twin rows of stalls, stacks of hay and burlap bags plump with what she imagined was ground corn. A corral joined the barn's east side.

Jenna turned her attention back to her new home and forced herself to see the possibilities—rockers on a tidy porch, planters filled with flowers and curtains in the windows.

"It's lovely," she managed to murmur.

He cleared his throat. "I'm building a bigger house up on the hill. It'll be ready before winter. Children need space."

Her cheeks burned pink.

Babies in the summer.

Pappy hurried out the front door and down the steps before she could summon a response. "About time you got here." The old man reached for the baby.

Jenna handed her over without hesitation. "She'll be hungry when she wakes."

"Already got her milk mixed and warming on the stove," he said.

"Are you sure she's not too much trouble?" Jenna asked.

Pappy adjusted Kate's blanket, careful she didn't get chilled in the evening air. "Ha! You'll be lucky if I give her back."

Jenna watched Pappy carry Kate inside, marveling at the way he had taken to her. "He's really good with her."

Rowe tied off the reins, set the brake on the buckboard and hopped down. "I reckon he misses his own children."

"Where are they?"

"Dead. Lost his three boys in the war and his wife and daughter to fever."

"How awful."

Rowe wrapped his hands around Jenna's narrow waist and lifted her to the ground. "He never talks much about it. Until today, I didn't realize he liked children so much. Seems our girl turns his insides to mush.''

Our girl.

Overcome by the simply spoken words, Jenna couldn't summon a response. She stared up at him, fresh tears glistening in her eyes.

Rowe stood stock-still. ''Let me show you inside,'' he said gruffly.

''I'd like that.''

With his hand pressed to the small of her back, he guided her to the main room. Two rockers and a chair sat next to a large stone hearth, where a fire blazed. A tattered rug warmed the floor and on the mantel hung the head of a grizzly bear, stuffed and mounted. A thick coating of dust covered the furniture, and the smell of smoke and men hung in the air. The place was in desperate need of cleaning.

Rowe nodded toward a door near the hearth. ''Let me show you to your room, so you can wash up.''

Jenna unclasped her cape. ''That sounds wonderful.''

He followed her to the threshold of a midsize bedroom. A wood stove hugged the left wall and a large bearskin rug covered the wood-plank floor. Next to the rug stood a rocker and a cradle.

Jenna walked over to the baby's bed and knelt

beside it. She touched the delicate spindles, marveling at their smoothness. "It's lovely."

Rowe leaned against the doorjamb, his arms folded over his chest. "I ordered it special, along with the bed."

"Bed?" Jenna glanced up at the large mahogany bed, surprised she'd not noticed it right off. It had four posters that nearly touched the low ceiling, and a fluffy down mattress. The fine bed was covered with freshly laundered sheets, horse blankets and two overstuffed pillows.

She stood and ran her fingers over the scratchy coverlet. A man's work shirt hung on one poster and a large pair of worn boots peeked out from under the bed.

Suddenly, the room grew smaller and the bed much, much larger as she realized where she was. "This is your room?"

He closed the bedroom door with a soft click. "Yes."

She snatched her hand from the bed as if it were made of hot coals. "Nice bed."

"It's an extravagance," he said. "It only arrived two weeks ago, but I've already gotten spoiled by it."

She managed a smile. "Could you show me where I will be sleeping for the next four weeks?"

"You'll sleep in here."

"I don't want to put you out."

"You won't."

"But where will you sleep?"

"Here."

Her face paled. Worried that Rowe wouldn't keep to their bargain, she stammered, "But I—I thought you said you'd give me a month."

His eyes gleamed with a sense of humor she hadn't suspected. "I said I wouldn't make love to you for a month. I didn't say anything about not sharing a bed with you."

"Sleep together?" she croaked. She didn't sound the least bit sophisticated or worldly, as a real widow might. In fact, she sounded downright skittish.

Rowe pulled off his hat and gloves and tossed them in the chair. "We *are* married."

"I know, but I think separate beds would be best for both of us. Four weeks isn't that long."

"There's no other bed in the house, and my years of sleeping out in the open are over."

"What about the barn?" she said hopefully. "Fresh hay can be so soft and fluffy."

He took a step forward. "The nights are getting cold."

As he wrapped his long fingers around the bedpost, she studied his sinewy muscles. She retreated a step. "You look pretty hardy to me. The brisk air wouldn't hurt you a bit."

A grin tugged at the corner of his mouth as he stepped closer. "My bones are getting too brittle." His wide shoulders said otherwise.

She stepped back again, this time bumping into the nightstand. The lantern sitting on it rattled, and she was forced to right it before it toppled over. "What about the bunkhouse? I'm sure there's a bed for you there, and I'll bet it's nice and warm."

"And full of cowhands. I'll never hear the end of it if I spend my wedding night with my men."

Jenna nibbled her bottom lip. "Then perhaps I can sleep out in the living room in front of the fire."

He blocked her path. "That wouldn't be right."

An unreasonable panic churned inside her. "Oh, I don't mind. I'm so tired tonight." She yawned to emphasize her point. "I will sleep like the dead." She tried to step around him.

He laid his hands on her shoulders and rubbed her collarbone with his thumb. "Jenna, you're sleeping with me tonight."

Her insides tightened. "Oh?" she said. Her imperious tone belied her growing fear.

He wasn't the least bit intimidated. "I promised that I would not make love to you for a month and I never break a promise."

"That's good to know," she said, her voice high-pitched now.

"I want you to get used to the feel of my body against yours."

A jolt of energy snaked down her spine. The room grew hot, the air thick. She'd never seen a man in a nightshirt, let alone felt his body spooned behind hers at night. It all seemed so unbearably intimate. She stared down at her feet, studying her shoes.

He captured her chin, tilted her head back and stared at her, silent and searching. "It's been a long time, hasn't it?"

"Since what?"

"You made love."

"Made love?" she said. She moistened her lips, embarrassed to be speaking of such things. "Yes, it's been awhile."

"Don't worry, it will be fine between us."

"I'm not worried!"

Rowe urged her toward him. His touch was tender, yet filled with power. She stood still, unable to take her eyes off his lips. As he bent his head toward her, she didn't retreat.

He gathered her up in his arms and pressed his lips to hers. He plunged his tongue into her mouth, and she rose up on tiptoe and accepted him without thinking. His touch seemed to have the same dizzying effect it had had at the hotel. Her breathing sped up; her heart raced.

With one arm he pinned her against his chest as he kissed her. His other hand slid over her breast and cupped it gently. He teased her nipple through the wool fabric, coaxing it into a soft peak.

Excitement and worry collided. Jenna felt herself slipping into a maelstrom of uncharted emotions. Her body pulsed with unfamiliar wanting, and she couldn't seem to summon a clear thought.

Rowe withdrew from her, nipped her bottom lip with his white teeth before he nuzzled her cheek with his rough whiskers. A thousand tiny shivers made her tingle inside.

"We're supposed to wait," she whispered breathless.

"Tell me to stop and we will."

"Stop," she whispered.

"Are you sure?"

No. "Yes."

He released her and shoved his fingers through his hair. Passion still darkened his eyes.

Now what were they supposed to do?

Kate's piercing cry shattered the clumsy silence.

The baby's voice echoed in the house. Jenna couldn't quite believe that she'd so completely abandoned her sensibilities. She'd never been overtaken with passion before. Of the Winslow sisters, she'd always been the calm, controlled one. Victoria had been the dramatic one, the one who'd flirted shamelessly with men. Everyone might have expected Victoria to end up in the wilds of Colorado aching for a man she barely knew.

But not Jenna.

Yet here she was.

Jenna had read thousands of books in her life, but none explained what was going on inside her. She'd always prided herself on knowing something about every topic, yet now she was at a complete loss.

She raised a trembling hand to smooth her chignon as she made a wide circle around Rowe and hurried out of the bedroom. She found Pappy bouncing a squawking Kate on his shoulder. "What's wrong?"

Pappy shook his head as he jostled the red-faced infant. "I fed her, but she don't seem to be happy with me one bit."

Jenna took Kate from him and laid the child over her shoulder. The babe's cries instantly slowed to whimpers. "It's been a long day for Kate," she said, swaying back and forth. "A warm bath and a good night's sleep are all she needs."

"We've got a tub," Rowe said from behind her. "I can draw a bath for you, if you like."

He'd taken off his range jacket and leaned

against the doorjamb with his arms folded across his chest. His hips were lean, his waist narrow. The sight of him made her mouth water.

Heat colored her cheeks as she patted Kate's backside. "Please, don't go to any trouble on my account."

Rowe walked up to her, gently cupped Kate's head in his large hand. He radiated energy, strength and tenderness. "No trouble."

Jenna's cheeks felt rough where his beard had rubbed, and his masculine scent still clung to her. Her mouth went dry.

She dragged her gaze up to Rowe's gray eyes, which sparked with fire. "Thank you."

"You're welcome, Jenna," he said silkily, and swaggered out of the room.

Horrified, Jenna realized Rowe knew that all he had to do was stare at her and she'd melt.

And to think she was a fine and proper lady who'd always followed the rules. Yet here she was, wanting Rowe Mercer more than it was right for a woman to want a man, even if he was her husband.

"You look like you ain't feeling well," Pappy said.

Jenna started as if she'd been caught with her hand in the cookie jar. "I'm fine."

Pappy laughed. "And pigs can fly."

* * *

Two hours later, Rowe paced the kitchen floor. He'd heated bathwater for Jenna and Kate, and left them in his room so they could clean up in privacy. He'd expected they wouldn't be more than a half hour, but they'd been cloistered behind closed doors for over two hours, and his patience was wearing thin. He had to be up before dawn, and he wanted to get to bed—with Jenna.

"How long does it take for a woman to bathe?" he growled.

Pappy leaned back in his chair and puffed on a pipe. Smoke swirled around his head. "Can take a spell."

"She's been in there forever. Hell, she wasn't even that dirty to begin with."

"I reckon women got more to wash than men. And then there is the youngun."

The idea of Jenna soaking naked in a tub drove Rowe to distraction. He clenched his teeth. He wanted to give her her privacy, wanted to give her a month, but damn it all, he wanted her.

This hunger he had for her threatened to shatter his well-ordered world. He'd worked hard to put his barbarous bounty-hunting past behind him and remake himself into a respected rancher. But every time he looked at Jenna, primal longings took over. He would not be satisfied until she lay naked under him, her eyes clouded with passion.

He glared at the closed door separating them. "I don't like being shut out of my own room."

Pappy puffed on his pipe. "The only lock in this house is on the front door. If you're so hell-bent on going in your room, then go."

The old man was right. What was he waiting for? He'd said he wouldn't make love to her for four weeks—and, by God, he'd keep his word. He wasn't so uncivilized that he couldn't carry on a civil conversation with his wife. And he'd never promised anything about not looking at her. "I believe I will."

With as much casualness as he could summon, he strode out of the kitchen to the bedroom. When he reached the door, he froze at the sound of splashing water.

Images of Jenna swirled through his mind. He pictured her blond ringlets, unpinned, freshly washed and draped over silky breasts moist with glistening beads of water.

Rowe stifled a groan. He heard another splash, followed by a throaty, utterly feminine laugh.

The next month was gonna be the longest in his life.

He let out a sigh and knocked on the door. "It's Rowe."

"Come in," Jenna said, sounding startled.

Rowe opened the door, but stopped abruptly at

the threshold. The scene before him nearly knocked him over.

Jenna knelt next to the tub, holding a naked baby Kate kicking and squirming over the water. His wife wore a rich, sapphire-colored dressing gown. Her blond locks, damp from her bath, were braided loosely and hung over her shoulder. Beads of water glistened on the tops of her breasts, exposed by the V opening at the front of her robe.

Rowe swallowed, wishing he'd stayed in the kitchen. This scene would hound him for the next thirty days. His mind turned to the pond a couple of hundred yards from the house. It was usually ice-cold by this time of year, and just the thing to cure his randy nature. "How about I come back later," he said.

"No, stay please. I need to bathe Kate, but I can't seem to figure out how I'm going to hold on to her and soap her down at the same time." She gifted him with a radiant smile that pierced his soul.

He cleared his throat. "What do you want me to do?"

She blew a stray curl off her face. "If you could just hold her, I can wash her."

Kate kicked her chubby legs and gurgled as she stared up at him. She blew a spit bubble and grinned.

He chuckled, relaxing. "How can I say no to that?" He strode across the room, then knelt down on the other side of the tub.

Jenna handed the flailing, naked infant to him. "Hold her under the arms. She'll be slippery once she's wet."

When he took the child, her head wobbled a bit, but her eyes were wide as she stared up at him. Struck by how fragile and trusting she was, he tightened his grip, fearing she'd slip from his fingers. "She's no bigger than a flea."

"She's stronger and faster than she looks."

Kate kicked her foot against the water and arched her back.

Laughter rumbled in Rowe's chest. "I think you're right." He pictured Kate riding a pony, her blond curls bobbing around her face and smiling blue eyes. He'd buy her a pony in the spring.

Pride warmed his heart as he lowered the wriggling baby. Kate cooed and splashed her palms in the water.

Jenna smiled at Kate, then dunked the soap in the water. "Who's my big girl?"

The sliver of soap Jenna used smelled faintly of roses, and Rowe realized she must have brought the luxury from Alexandria. He made a mental note to order more for her the next time he was in town.

"She'll be crawling before we know it," Jenna said easily. "She's already rolling and trying to push up on her hands and knees."

As Jenna washed the child, she spoke easily, without the signs of strain that had marred her smooth skin most of today. The bond between them was still fragile, but she was beginning to trust him, feel at ease with him.

A spring coiled inside his gut. He'd had his share of women—hurdy-gurdy girls and a widow woman or two. He'd given as good as he'd gotten, but those temporary unions had been based only on physical need. He had always walked away without a backward glance, priding himself on the fact that he didn't need anybody.

But his connection to Jenna was different. It ran deeper than hastily spoken marriage vows or sexual need—though there was a healthy dose of that pounding in his blood.

There was something more between them, but he couldn't say what. He did know that not having her in his life was now unthinkable.

The insight offered little comfort and spawned fresh worries. For the first time, he wasn't in control.

And it scared the hell out of him.

Chapter Five

As Jenna rinsed the soap from the baby's tiny body, her fingers brushed Rowe's. Energy snapped through her fingertips, toppling her emotions like apples from a rickety cart. Suddenly, her light mood evaporated and the room stilled.

Moments passed before she even dared steal a peek at Rowe. But when she did, she discovered he was staring at her, his gaze dark and unwavering. He had felt it, too. For an instant, there was only the beating of her heart and Rowe's deep, even breaths.

Kate kicked and wriggled, smacking her toes in the water. The child's squeal of delight broke Jenna's trance.

She gathered her wits and made quick work of rinsing the baby, then picked up a towel. "Hand her to me and I'll get her nightclothes on."

Rowe gingerly placed the infant in Jenna's towel-draped hands, then watched as she carried the child to the bed, dried her off and dressed her in a cotton gown. Jenna struggled with the tiny mother of pearl buttons that lined the front of the tiny garment. She was clumsier tonight than she had been the very first time she'd dressed the child.

With her task complete, Jenna laid Kate in the cradle, then kissed her on the forehead. Kate lay content, her wide eyes blinking slowly as she stared up at Jenna and chewed on her fist.

"Now it's time for Miss Kate to lie down," Jenna said, grinning at the child.

Kate yawned and smiled lazily.

Rowe rose to his feet and slowly dried his hands on the towel Jenna had used on Kate. "We've all had a long day and could use a good night's sleep."

Jenna looked at the large bed longingly. Its plump mattress and down pillows beckoned her aching body, but she couldn't summon the nerve to climb into bed with Rowe. She closed the lapels of her robe. "I thought perhaps I'd sit up and read for a while. For some reason I'm not a bit sleepy."

He frowned. "The dark smudges under your eyes say otherwise."

"Dark circles and lack of sleep come with

babies. I generally read a little each night before I go to bed.''

He glanced in the crib. Kate's eyes dropped and fluttered shut. "Looks like she's just about asleep now."

"She could wake and be frightened of her new surroundings. I'd best stay up." Jenna retrieved a leather-bound book from her valise, not bothering to look at the spine, and took a seat in the rocker by the hearth. "Why don't you get into bed? I'll be along shortly."

She stifled a yawn and offered him one of her brightest smiles, then opened the book. Her scratchy, tired eyes could barely focus on a single word, but reading was the only reasonable delay tactic she had. She prayed Rowe would soon grow tired and fall asleep. Once he was out for the night, she'd slip into her side of the bed.

She settled on a random page as Rowe shrugged off his vest and hung it on a bedpost. She focused on the book, but her mind kept drifting to Rowe. She reread the same sentence three times but couldn't make sense of it.

Rowe sat on the edge of the bed and yanked off a scuffed boot. He dropped it to the floor. "I'll be gone most of the day tomorrow," he offered as he tugged off the second boot and set it next to the other. "I should be back around sunset."

She turned an unread page. "Don't worry about us. We're used to getting along by ourselves."

"Pappy will be here."

"Good." She glanced up at Rowe just as he unfastened the buttons on his shirt. She moistened her dry lips. "You look tired. You should get to sleep."

"I'll wait for you."

She waved away his offer. "Don't put yourself out on my account. I could be up for a while."

He pulled his shirt over his head. "How long?"

Lantern light glistened on bronzed skin and a thick mat of hair that tapered down to his narrow waist. He reached for his belt buckle.

Jenna watched his fingers as he unfastened the silver buckle. She'd never seen a man unclothed before and, though shocked by her own thoughts, was curious. "Not long. An hour or two."

She heard denim sliding over muscle. Curiosity got the better of her and she glanced up. To her awe, she realized he didn't wear long johns. Treated to her first look at a naked man, Jenna couldn't stop her jaw from falling open.

As if he'd been chiseled from marble, his body conjured images of Greek gods and mythic warriors. Dry mouthed, she surveyed Rowe's naked form, from his well-muscled shoulders to his manhood.

"Curiosity killed the cat," he said.

Her gaze skittered to his face and the wry grin that curled the corner of his full lips.

Please, Lord, let the floorboards swallow me up now.

"I—I—I'm sorry." She jumped to her feet so fast her book thumped to the floor. She decided as she whirled toward the hearth that the bed was the *last* place she was going to sleep tonight. The rocker was stiff but would do just fine.

She pressed trembling hands to her hot cheeks as she stared at the firelight dancing on the folds of her dressing gown.

Her mother had never explained the bedroom goings-on between men and women, always saying that task fell to Jenna's husband. Thanks to a few bits of information from Victoria, she had a sense of what happened, but there were key details she wasn't exactly clear about.

Right now, she'd trade her last nickel for an experienced woman's advice.

Rowe's steady footsteps padded across the floor toward her. She could feel him standing behind her, but didn't dare turn and look at him. She hugged her arms around her chest.

He laid his hands on her shoulders and she cringed. "Jenna, you're gonna have to get used to the sight of me in my where-with-all."

"It's just that I'm very modest."

"I'm not."

She rolled her eyes. "I guessed."

"You must have seen your first husband naked."

"I certainly did not!"

He mumbled something about city men being fools, then leaned closer to her, his lips grazing her ear. "Come to bed."

"As soon as you put on your nightshirt."

"I don't wear one."

"Of course you don't." Chewing on her bottom lip, she realized she felt a bit hysterical. "I need a few minutes. I'd like to finish the chapter I'm reading."

He touched her curls, now almost completely dry. "Five minutes, then it's lights out." He gave her shoulders a gentle squeeze and strode over to the bed. She heard him slide under the covers and plump up his pillow.

Jenna stared into the fire an extra second or two. The flames overheated her skin, but she didn't move right away. She wanted to make certain he had enough time to cover up.

Finally, she took a step back and, careful to keep her gaze on the floor, sat down again, picked up her book and blindly opened the novel.

"Must be a good book," he said.

"It's my favorite."

"What's it about?"

"It's an adventure."

"Interesting?"

"Riveting."

A moment of silence passed, and she thought that maybe he'd lost interest and would settle in for the night.

"Jenna?"

She started. "Yes?" This time she dared to look in his direction.

Rowe had tucked his hands behind his head, and his eyes twinkled with laughter. "Your book is upside down."

Jenna nearly groaned. So much for sophistication. With as much dignity as she could muster she turned the book around.

"Jenna, time to come to bed."

"I'm really not sleepy."

"Now," he said softly.

"But—"

He reached for the sheet covering him. "Do I need to come and get you?"

Images of him standing naked flashed in her mind. She hopped to her feet and tossed her book in the chair. "Stay put. I'm coming."

He relaxed back against the pillows, staring at her, waiting.

Jenna walked slowly toward her side of the bed, careful to keep as much distance as she could between herself and him. She paused by the edge, drew in a deep breath and kicked off her bedroom slippers.

She reached for the belt of her robe as Rowe rolled onto his side and faced her. He propped his head up on his hand, clearly delighting in the sight of her. She decided to keep her robe on, craving its extra protection.

"This is one fine bed." She poked the pillow with her finger and tested the firmness of the mattress. "Very fine indeed." She patted the mattress again.

"You're stalling."

"I know."

Her honesty made him laugh. "I don't bite."

"I know," she repeated, more out of politeness than conviction.

Rowe tossed back the blankets on her side of the bed and waited. "Come on," he coaxed.

Mustering the shreds of her courage, she climbed into bed, careful to stay as close to the edge as possible. Quickly, she tossed the covers over her body and rolled on her back. The icy sheets stung her bare feet, making it more difficult to relax as she stared at the ceiling, her hands clasped tightly on her chest.

"You're not going to take off your robe?"

"I'm a little chilly tonight."

"I can warm you up."

"No, no! The robe is quite adequate."

Rowe turned toward his nightstand and blew out the lantern. The room went dark except for the firelight flickering on the hearth.

When he faced her again, his face was bathed in shadows. He made no move to touch her. "Your spine's so straight it's liable to snap."

Jenna flexed her fingers. "I'm perfectly relaxed."

"Then scoot toward me."

She nearly bolted out of bed. "What?"

He didn't ask a second time. Instead he reached out through the darkness and pulled her toward him until she lay on her side, her back against his body. He draped his large arm over her waist and hugged her against him. "That's better."

Jenna tried to squirm free. "I don't know about this."

"It's where you belong."

"Aren't we rushing things?"

He rested his chin on the top of her head. "We're married."

Jenna wanted to scream that she was a virgin. That she had no business being in his bed and that this was all so unbearably intimate. That until yesterday her experience with men amounted to demure kisses and hand-holding!

But she couldn't say any of that, yet. She needed time to figure out how she was going to break the news of the scandal that had brought her to him.

Trapped with nowhere to go, Jenna lay cradled in Rowe's arms. Slowly, his deep even breaths coupled with the warmth of his body took effect.

The coil of nerves lodged in her stomach eased a fraction and her eyelids got just a little heavier. Alexandria and her family seemed so far away.

"Rowe?" she whispered, afraid he might have fallen asleep.

"Yes." His voice sounded awake, alert.

She swirled her fingertip on the rough coverlet. "Why didn't you marry a woman from Saddler Creek?"

"Not many marriageable women in these parts."

"Why'd you run your ad in the Alexandria paper?"

"Alexandria, Denver, Chicago, St. Louis—I ran ads in all their papers."

"Oh." A needle of jealously poked her insides. "You must have had a lot of responses to your ad."

"Half a dozen."

"I bet they all had ranch experience."

"Uh-huh."

She felt woefully inadequate. "Why'd you pick me when you knew I'd never lived on a ranch before?"

"I liked your handwriting."

She laughed. "You're joking."

"No," he said seriously. "I could tell right off you were a woman of breeding and education. I want my sons growing up to be smart, educated men."

Babies in the summer.

"Oh."

He pressed his palm against her flat stomach. "You're as slim as a reed. It's hard to imagine you've had a child."

She held her breath, unsure of what to say.

"Was childbirth hard for you?"

Her chest tightened. "No."

"Good."

The lie weighed heavily inside her, like a rock. Worry after worry knotted her stomach. Soon her lies would carry her past the point of winning Rowe's forgiveness.

He slid his hand down her thigh. "Why'd you move out here?"

"I wanted to remarry."

"That's not what I mean." He stroked her leg. "A woman with servants and a fancy upbringing doesn't need to move to a place like Saddler Creek to find a good husband. Seems to me the fellows in Alexandria would have been lined up to marry you.''

"Not really."

"Why not? You never said in your letters why you wanted to leave the East."

"Alexandria may seem big compared to Saddler Creek, but in many ways it's a small town. There was some gossip about my family," she hedged. "Word spread quickly and before long people didn't want to associate with us." She waited, tight as a bowstring, for the next question.

"This gossip have anything to do with you?"

"I've nothing to be ashamed of."

"That doesn't answer my question."

She sighed. "My parents had a lot of debts," she said truthfully. "They'd spent heavily this last year, expecting their investment to pay well. When it failed them, they were forced to leave town quickly to avoid their creditors and possibly jail."

"What's their debt got to do with you?"

"Guilt by association, I suppose."

"Where are they now?"

"New York, I think."

He draped his arm protectively over her waist. "You don't know for certain?"

Her parents' indifference had been a part of her

life since she was a child, and it no longer troubled her. "They'll send word eventually. They always do."

"Why would they leave you behind?" Anger had crept into his voice.

"It was easier. They can travel much faster alone."

She rubbed her fingertips over the back of his hand. "When my parents left, and I discovered no one would help, I prayed for a solution. The next day I saw your ad and I responded."

"You answer any other ads?" Tension edged his words.

"Just yours."

He relaxed. "You must have been desperate to take such a chance."

"I was."

"You ever wonder if you're gonna regret coming so far away from what's familiar?"

"I won't," she said, with as much conviction as she could muster.

Rowe didn't respond, and lapsed into a brooding silence. They lay together, their bodies giving and drawing heat. His scent was a rich combination of tobacco and musk. It enveloped her, and she couldn't help but notice how it was so unlike Everett's heavy, sweet cologne.

Everything about the two men was as opposite

as night and day. Before their troubles, Everett had been witty, charming, so easy to be with, and at one time she'd felt that she'd known him as well as anybody. He'd been kind to her when her parents never had. But in the end Everett's weakness and deceit had proved that he was just like her parents.

Rowe wasn't the type of man to court her with honeyed words or expensive gifts. He spoke his mind, and she had a sense that she would always know where she stood with him. Still, there was so much she didn't know about him—so many unanswered questions.

But unlike anyone else, he'd opened his home to Kate and her, and for that she'd always be grateful.

She stifled a yawn. She was so tired and the bed felt so good. Maybe she'd close her eyes just for a minute or two.

Jenna snuggled her bottom closer to Rowe, savoring his warmth. Her eyelids grew heavier until finally they drifted closed. As sleep overtook her, she had a vague sensation of Rowe gently touching her hair. Oddly, the feeling eased her worries.

Just as she slipped into a deep sleep, she heard him sigh and felt his large hand cup her breast.

Her eyelids popped open.

What if she fell asleep and Rowe took the opportunity to take advantage?

The fire crackled and hissed. Could she trust that she'd be safe from his advances while she slept? She shifted, uncomfortable with his nearness.

"What's wrong?" He sounded half-asleep.

She drew circles on the sheet with her fingertip. "If I fell asleep, let my guard down, you could, well...you know, and I might not ever know it."

He snuggled closer. "When I make love to you, Jenna, you're going to know it."

Chapter Six

Jenna didn't want to wake up. And she wouldn't have if the bright sunlight hadn't nudged her away from slumber and a wonderful dream filled with music, laughter and one perfect, bygone moment with Everett.

She draped an arm over her eyes, trying to shield them from the light. But the sunshine prodded her toward consciousness until finally she abandoned the remnants of her dream.

Disoriented and annoyed, she pushed herself up and rubbed her eyes. Bit by bit, her mind sharpened enough so she understood she wasn't in her bed in Alexandria. The realization didn't bother her. In fact, she felt safe.

She indulged in a long, deep stretch that loosened the kinks from her arms and back. The bed felt so good, so warm. Perhaps, if she lay back against the pillows, she could steal a few more moments, recapture some of her dream.

As she eased onto the pillow, memories of yesterday and the last six months struck her in one blinding flash. She shot back up, fully awake.

She was married!

Jenna's gaze vaulted to her husband's side of the bed. Mercifully, he was gone.

She buried her face in her hands, rubbing her eyes. Lord above, her life had changed so much so fast. Victoria, her parents, Everett—all gone, and in their place Kate and Rowe.

Kate! Where was Kate? The baby always woke her well before dawn. Springing to her feet, Jenna ignored the chilly floorboards and hurried past her unpacked luggage to the cradle. The baby was there, lying so still that Jenna feared something might be wrong with her.

Gently, she laid her hand on the baby's chest and counted her steady breaths. One. Two. Three. The babe was sleeping deeper than she ever had, but she was fine. Jenna touched her downy hair. A little angel, born to such turmoil, Kate slept without a care in the world, as if she understood Jenna's marriage to Rowe had brought stability to their lives.

Jenna shoved a shaky hand through her own hair. Like Kate, she, too, had been exhausted and

in desperate need of sleep. Bone weary as she'd
been last night, she doubted anything could have
woken her up, not even...

When I make love to you, Jenna, you'll know it.

She could feel the blood drain from her head as
she imagined his hands on her.

Her heart racing, she peeked inside her nightgown at her body. It didn't look any different. She
didn't feel any different.

When I make love to you, Jenna, you'll know it.

"You're being silly," she whispered. "He gave
you his word."

Groaning, Jenna sat on the edge of the bed.
She'd not think about *that* right now. It was a
month away. Thirty days. Seven hundred and
twenty hours. Plenty of time to get to know her
husband.

A fraction calmer, she let her gaze skim her new
bedroom, now bathed in daylight. A half-dozen
split logs burned on the hearth, warming the chilly
room and adding the only real bit of charm.

Without a flower vase or extra pillow to warm
it up, the room looked harsher in the bright light.
Soon her trunks would arrive and she'd be able to
add a homey touch here and there. Today she
would concentrate on unpacking the few bags she
had brought with her on the train.

Her stomach growled and she realized she'd not

eaten since breakfast yesterday. Hungry and ready to start her new life, Jenna decided she'd dress and eat before Kate woke.

Rising, she crossed to her valise and pulled out a sapphire-blue dress made of wool, with a high neckline and long sleeves. The dress was one of her plainest, and Jenna had packed it certain it would do. But having seen how rugged her surroundings truly were, she felt overdressed.

Refusing to worry, she donned the garment, crossed to the porcelain pitcher and basin resting on the bureau, and washed the sleep from her eyes.

Turning to the bed, she smoothed the sheets and blankets and then fluffed her pillow. When she reached for Rowe's pillow, she noted his masculine scent still clung to the soft fabric. She raised the pillow to her nose and drank in the aroma. Her pulse quickened.

Quickly she laid his pillow next to hers. Then Jenna checked Kate again, before she opened the door and stepped into the main room.

Like the bedroom, this large, rectangular room was bare to the point of being Spartan, but her mind was already teeming with ideas—curtains in the windows, flowers and perhaps a new braided rug. She walked toward the central hearth, where another fire burned. She held out her palms, letting the heat soak into her skin. Sighing, she savored a moment of relaxed contentment. Everything was going to be fine.

A shotgun blast shattered the morning calm.

Jenna ducked, her heart hammering in her chest. "Rowe! Pappy!"

Seconds passed but no answer came. Had they left her here alone? Keeping her head low, she started back toward her room and Kate, then heard Rowe's angry voice from outside the house.

"Boone, I've said all I need to say," he shouted.

Knowing Rowe was close gave her the courage to unfold her body and rise. Likely there was nothing to worry about. This was the wilderness, after all, not Alexandria. The dime novels said people fired guns here all the time.

She hurried to the front door, eased it open and stepped out onto the porch. She saw four riders in profile facing Rowe, who stood at the entrance to the barn. The riders wore weathered, dusty clothes and faded range coats tucked behind their guns. Hats shadowed their eyes.

Rowe's body was rigid with fury, his hand resting on his gun as he squared off with the men. Beside Rowe stood Pappy, a smoking shotgun in hand. Two other cowhands flanked Pappy and Rowe, guns drawn.

Even from this distance, Jenna could see that her

husband's face wore a savage expression, feral almost.

All the men, Rowe included, were so focused on each other that they didn't notice her as she closed the front door.

One of the four riders, stocky and thick necked, glanced at the grizzled men behind him. "I come to talk, Mercer."

"I'm not in the mood for conversation, Boone," Rowe said, his teeth clenched.

The man called Boone leaned forward in his saddle. "You owe me, Mercer."

"I don't owe you anything."

Boone's eyes narrowed. "You ruined my life."

"You did that all by yourself," Pappy said. Every bit of kindness Jenna had seen in the old man's face had vanished.

Boone snorted. "Mercer, somebody's gonna knock you and that old man down a peg one of these days."

"It won't be you," Rowe said.

One of Boone's gang reached for his gun. Before the gun cleared leather, Rowe drew his own gun and shot the man in the hand. The stranger yelped, cussed and cupped his bleeding fingers.

Jenna's stomach flip-flopped as she shrank back. She'd read about rough men who called the West home. She'd drunk in every detail about desperadoes and bounty hunters and their dangerous lives, but she wasn't prepared for the reality of this. The dark side of Rowe was so unlike the man she'd been with last night. He was a stranger to her.

"Get off my land before I shoot you, Boone," Rowe ordered.

Boone glanced around the yard, where a gentle wind was kicking up the dust. "This ranch is your life."

Silent, Rowe remained alert, gun drawn.

"We've had a drought this summer," Boone continued. "The land's like tinder. You know the Thompson ranch burned last week."

Rowe's hand tightened around his gun handle. "My place burns, you die. That's a promise."

Boone grinned. "Iron Man Mercer. Untouchable. No weaknesses."

Rowe's narrowed.

"Even iron melts at the right temperature," Boone said.

In two strides, Rowe closed the gap separating them. With one hand, he grabbed the man by the coat collar and dragged him off his horse. Rowe pressed the point of the gun to Boone's temple. Three sets of guns snapped free from holsters and zeroed in on Rowe. Pappy raised his shotgun and the cowhands beside him raised their rifles.

Rowe cocked his pistol. "Tell 'em to toss their guns down. Now!"

Boone paled. "You don't scare me."

Rowe jabbed the tip of his gun into Boone's temple. "Then you're not as smart as I figured. One, two…"

"Drop your guns!" Boone shouted.

The men hesitated, unwilling to part with their firearms. Tense seconds passed and Rowe glared at his opponents. Any one of the men could shoot him down, yet he seemed angry at the thought, not scared.

Expecting a gunfight to erupt at any minute, Jenna stepped back until her spine pressed against the front door. Her gaze skittered between Rowe and Boone's men.

Rowe started to squeeze the trigger.

"Drop your damn guns!" Boone yelled.

One by one, the men released their pistols and dropped them in the dirt. Pappy collected each one and tossed it into the barn, out of reach.

Jenna breathed a sigh of relief.

Rowe yanked Boone's gun from his holster, then pushed him toward his horse. "Get off my land."

Boone stumbled, righted himself and then took a moment to brush the dirt from his overcoat. As he reached for the reins of his horse, his gaze flickered toward the house and Jenna. He froze, staring at her as if he didn't quite believe what he saw. Then an oily smile curved the corners of his lips and he touched the brim of his hat.

"I heard you'd taken a wife, Mercer," Boone said casually. "But I didn't believe it."

Rowe's head jerked around. The rage that darkened his eyes made Jenna cringe. Never had anyone looked at her with such anger.

"I didn't realize she was such a pretty little thing," Boone said.

Rowe flexed his fingers, staring past Boone at Jenna. She was paralyzed, too frightened to move.

Chuckling, Boone mounted his horse. "Hope it doesn't get too rough for her out here."

"Go back inside," Rowe ordered Jenna.

Fearful, she stumbled into the house and closed the door. Her palms damp, she backed away across the room.

Seconds after she heard Boone and his men ride off, Rowe opened the front door. He closed it behind him with a loud bang.

Her knees wobbled and she raised her chin a notch, refusing to be frightened by her husband.

"Do you have any idea what you've done?" His voice was deadly quiet, menacing even.

"I didn't mean to interfere."

"You shouldn't have come outside."

"I heard the gunfire."

Rowe's jaw flexed as he visibly struggled to keep his temper in check. "From now on when riders show up unexpected, stay inside. No questions asked."

"Visitors are bound to come from time to time, and I don't see why I can't greet them."

"This is *my* land and *my* house and I expect everyone here to follow my orders. *Do you understand?*" His voice reverberated in the room. Kate started to cry.

Jenna could only stare at him in silent rebellion, shocked and hurt that he'd speak to her so rudely.

"Do you understand?"

She winced. Tears born of anger burned her throat. "Yes," she hissed.

"Good." He turned on his heel and left through the front door, once again slamming it behind him.

Jenna pressed her palms to her hot cheeks.

"Oh dear Lord," she whispered. "I've made a terrible mistake marrying Rowe Mercer."

Rowe reached the barn, then stopped and pressed the heels of his hands into his eyes. What the hell had set him off moments ago?

He dragged a shaking hand through his hair. He knew the answer. It had been fear that had ignited his temper.

He shouldn't have yelled at Jenna, but when that

son of a bitch Boone had leered at her, something dangerous and cold had unfurled inside of Rowe.

It wasn't Jenna's fault that she'd ventured onto the porch or witnessed what she had. Greeting visitors was what a good rancher's wife did. But that hadn't stopped him from unleashing on her wrath meant for Boone.

He yanked off his hat and wiped the sweat from his brow. He'd known her less than twenty-four hours, but the thought of losing her unsettled him completely. Boone had been right. He had a weakness.

Hat in hand, he turned and strode back to the house. He reached for the doorknob and twisted it. He had to make things right with Jenna.

He opened the door and strode toward their bedroom. He found her sitting next to Kate's crib, holding the baby on her shoulder. Her gaze darted up to his, her expressive face revealing the depth of her hurt.

Kate stirred and started to cry again. Automatically, Jenna patted the baby on the back and whispered soothingly in her ear.

He struggled to string together words that would make things right between them. Instead, he heard himself say, "I'm riding out to the south end of the property."

"Okay."

He flexed his fingers, irritated at his clumsiness, and advanced into the room. "I thought you might like to join me."

She took a step back. "No. T-thank you."

His jaw tensed as his gaze skimmed over her unpacked luggage. "Maybe it's best you stay close. You've got a lot of unpacking to do."

Jenna glanced around the room. "I'm not going to unpack."

His gut tightened. "What do you mean?"

"I don't think I can stay."

He couldn't speak, his gray eyes searing her pale, delicate features. The silence hung between them, as heavy and real as a stone wall.

"Colorado is not what I expected." He heard the tremor in her voice.

Disquiet, keen and sharp, jabbed him. "*I'm* not what you'd expected," he countered. He tossed his hat aside. Damn it, how had he messed things up so quickly? Jenna reminded him of a wounded doe, and he hated the fact that he'd been the cause of her fear. He forced his muscles to relax. He would have to move slowly if he were going to repair the damage between them. "What do you propose?"

"I should leave." The deadly calm of her voice shook him more than any threat Boone could muster. "There are other women, much stronger than me, who are better suited to this land—to you."

There are no other women like you.

The words were perched on the tip of his tongue, but remained unspoken. She had to know she was special, perfect. "I see."

"I've got a little of my own money," she rushed to say. "So I won't ask you for any."

Despite his vow to move cautiously, he advanced toward her, closing the distance between them in three strides. Gently, he laid his hands on her shoulders, trapping the baby between their bodies. His heart thundered in his chest as her gaze fluttered up to his. "I shouldn't have yelled at you. I'm used to firing orders at my men. It's gonna take me some time to change my style."

Her eyes glistened. "I can't expect you to change. You've done well because you are who you are. Which is exactly why I think I should leave. I'm just not suited to this life. I thought I could handle it, but I can't."

He captured a ringlet that had fallen loose from her ribbon, and wrapped it around his callused finger. "You aren't going anywhere," he said, steel in his voice.

He'd make it up to her. She'd soon see this was where she belonged.

She stepped back and straightened her shoulders. "That's for me to decide, not you."

"You made your decision when you spoke your vows yesterday."

"I didn't know what it was really like out here. I didn't expect guns, threats and trouble."

"I'm not letting you run off at the first sign of trouble."

"I'm not running. I'm being reasonable."

"Running is your style," he challenged.

Her cheeks flushed. "I don't run," she said, her voice tight.

He preferred her anger to her fear. "You ran from some kind of trouble in Alexandria."

Her body stilled. She didn't speak, but her gaze sharpened. He'd hit a nerve.

"You did run."

"I left for Kate's sake," she said. "Alexandria wasn't good for her."

"So this is all about *Kate?*"

"Yes."

There was more to what had happened back East than she was saying, but discovering that was for later. Now was about convincing her to stay.

"Alexandria might have been about *Kate,* but what's happening right here and now is about *us.*"

"It's too dangerous out here! You would have killed Boone if you'd had to."

"In a heartbeat. And I'd have dragged his dead body into town as an example to anyone else who thought they could come out here and threaten my family.''

"That's barbaric!"

"That's life out here."

"I can't live this way."

"We are married for better or for worse."

"I can't do it," she whispered.

He stepped toward her. "You can."

Tears welled in her eyes. "I'm not the kind of wife you need."

"You're the one I want."

He tilted her head back and forced her to meet his gaze. "Unpack your things, Jenna. You're not running away from me."

Chapter Seven

Jenna pushed away from Rowe and settled Kate in her crib before she turned and faced him. The steel in his voice had fueled her ire. "What if I don't agree?"

"For better or worse, Jenna."

"Yes, but—"

"No buts."

She *had* spoken vows. And it wasn't like her to crumple at the first sign of trouble. But she sensed anger hadn't driven Rowe's outburst. Fear had. Which of course was ridiculous. Rowe Mercer wasn't afraid of anything.

She folded her hands over her chest. "You don't have to be so bossy. I do listen when people explain things calmly and rationally."

Rowe expelled a frustrated sigh. "This land is unforgiving. The trail between here and town is lined with the unmarked graves of men who underestimated this country. I know because I buried most of them.''

She took a step closer to him, willing him to meet her halfway. ''Maybe I do have a lot to learn. But the only way I'm going to learn is if you talk to me, explain things rationally to me. What happened outside today? Who is Boone?''

Rowe stared down at her long, manicured fingers and frowned. ''It's my job to worry about the Boones of this world. Not yours.''

''How can I understand if you don't explain?''

''There's nothing to understand about Boone. He is my problem, not yours.''

''A real wife shares her husband's burdens.''

His gaze nailed her. ''You and I both know you're not a real wife to me yet.''

His harsh words stung. ''That's not fair. I told you I just needed a month.''

''Three weeks, six days,'' he corrected. ''But I wasn't talking about the bedroom just then.'' He leaned forward until their faces were only inches apart. ''You're holding some secret from me.''

Her knees nearly buckled. ''Why do you say that?''

''Deny it.''

''Alexandria is the p-past,'' she stammered. ''I'm talking about now.''

"I'm talking about trust."

She raised her chin. "I trust you."

"Do you?"

"Y-yes."

"Then why'd you leave Alexandria to marry a man like me?"

His question surprised her. "You've a lot to offer a wife."

"I've a hard life to offer. A woman doesn't leave high society for ranch life without good reason."

"Maybe I just wanted something different."

"Not this different." He took her hand in his and turned it over. He traced his callused finger down her lifeline, scowled at the smooth skin of her palm. "I was watching you while you were sleeping last night. The more I studied your face, the more I wondered why you chose me."

"You offered us a home."

"You could have gotten that in Alexandria. I can't believe you couldn't have found a husband."

Her chest tightened with worry. "I didn't want to stay in Alexandria."

"Why?"

She stared into his dark eyes and found herself filled with a deep-seated longing. She tried to tug her hand free and wished she could escape his scrutiny. "I just didn't belong anymore."

He didn't release her hand. "Don't run from me."

Rowe was right when he'd said running was her style. First from Alexandria, then the violence she'd just witnessed, and now the truth.

But running had kept Kate safe, and it worked when trust had failed. "Nothing happened."

The muscles in his jaw tensed. "Trust's a two-way street, Jenna. Until you can trust me with the past, don't expect me to trust you with my problems."

Her throat tightened with unexpected sadness. "So where does that leave us—living separate lives?"

Rowe stared down into her face for what seemed like forever. Then he cupped her face in his hands. "We may not trust each other yet, but we do have this."

He leaned forward and pressed his lips to hers, coaxing them open with his tongue. She struggled to remain detached, but a warm, delicious feeling spread through her limbs, turning them to jelly. She'd struggled to control her life for months now, but in Rowe's arms sweet chaos beckoned, and it frightened her to the bone.

Rowe pulled his lips from hers. She blinked, her lids heavy, and something deep inside of her shifted. She'd given her heart once and tasted bitter rejection. Yet here she was, clinging to a virtual stranger. "Don't make me care about you," she whispered, more to herself than him.

He laid his hands on her shoulders. "Is that so bad?"

She closed her eyes, her head reeling. "Caring wasn't part of our bargain."

He traced the line of her jaw with his thumb. "I'm willing to renegotiate."

"You're a dangerous man, Rowe Mercer."

A grin tugged at the corners of his mouth as he leaned a little closer. Before she could respond, he kissed her forehead and snatched up his hat. "Only in a good way."

An hour later, Jenna had fed Kate, tucked the child into her basket and ventured into the kitchen. She set the basket on the large round table and went to the wood-burning stove. There a coffeepot simmered near a plate of biscuits—Pappy's handiwork, she guessed.

Jenna poured a mug of hot coffee and picked up a biscuit. The coffee was strong and the biscuit filling.

With something in her stomach and distance from Rowe, Jenna's nerves settled enough for her to realize her threats of leaving were born out of hurt feelings, not fear. Calmer now, she focused on her new house and tackling the business of organizing the kitchen.

She set her dirty cup in the washtub, already filled with a dozen encrusted plates, then headed toward the pantry. As she peered into the darkened space, her nose wrinkled at the dust covering sacks of beans, flour and salt. Grimy canisters of lard and sugar sat open on the shelves next to partially washed mixing spoons, baking pans coated with old dough and a butter churn that looked as if it hadn't seen daylight in months. Mouse droppings littered the floor.

Jenna shook her head. "It'll take me the better part of the day to clean this mess."

During the months Jenna had been sequestered with Victoria, their parents had provided them with a small allowance, enough for rent and food, but not enough for servants. So Jenna had learned to gather eggs, churn butter, milk cows and cook simple meals. At the time the new responsibilities had been overwhelming, and she'd resented her parents for treating their daughters so heartlessly. Now she said a silent prayer of thanks for the basic skills.

She glanced back at Kate, who stared intently at her. "What do you say we have a look around the ranch first? We'll clean the pantry later. I know they've got a milk cow here, but do you think we're lucky enough to have a henhouse, Miss Kate?''

Kate gurgled. Laughing, Jenna tucked the baby on her hip and headed toward the back door. ''Let's enjoy some of that sunshine.''

She wrapped an extra blanket around Kate before stepping outside. The October day was chilly, the air fresh and crisp, and the scent of snow hung in the air.

Jenna drank in the peaceful sight of purple, snow-capped mountains standing in the distance. A gentle breeze teased the tops of the tall grasses, and the sun warmed her face. So unlike the crowded, smelly streets of Alexandria, this untamed land possessed the promise of a grand future.

Then Jenna recalled Boone's leering look. The memory of his presence marred the land's near perfection. Even the rose had thorns.

Shoving aside a niggling worry, she forced herself to think about her chores instead. She scanned the yard and to her delight spotted a chicken coop a few hundred paces from the house. Though weathered and sun-baked, the small building looked sturdy. Two roosters eyed her and clucked.

Jenna moved toward the coop, shifting the baby from one hip to the other. As she got closer, she realized she hadn't brought a basket with her. "How am I going to manage Kate and the eggs?"

"The Indian women use a cradleboard to hold their little ones," Pappy said from behind her. "Keeps their hands free for chores."

Startled, Jenna turned to find the old man. He still carried his shotgun, but the hard edge had vanished from his weathered features.

"A cradleboard?" she said smiling.

Pappy winked at Kate. "Contraption that holds the baby. It's strapped to the ma's back so her hands are always free. They're right handy." He leaned his shotgun against the chicken coop, pulled off his work gloves and held out his hands to Kate. The baby leaned toward him happily. "I'll make one for you, if you like."

"That would be wonderful, if it's not too much trouble."

Pappy grinned. "Ain't no trouble."

Jenna peered into the henhouse. "I want to start making myself useful around here."

"Never a shortage of work."

Creating a pocket in the folds of her skirts, Jenna ventured into the chicken coop. "Do you take care of the house?"

"Yes, but I ain't much of a homemaker."

Jenna reached under a brown, plump hen. The hen clucked and ruffled her feathers, but Pappy spoke a few words to the creature and she settled down. With Pappy at her side, Jenna pulled out an egg. "I'm not much of one, either, but if it doesn't offend you, I can take over running the house."

"Don't bother me at all. I know the ranch hands won't mind a different person stirring the dinner pot."

She remembered the pot of stew. "How many ranch hands do you cook for?"

A rooster crowed and flapped his wings, but Pappy shooed him away. "Seeing as it's winter, there's just Rowe, me and two other fellows. Come spring, fifteen more men will return to help with the roundups and branding. They stay through the fall. Fact is, they just left about a week ago."

Jenna dug three more eggs out from under hens. "Spring should be enough time for me to get my bearings."

"You'll catch on fast."

She paused, staring at the collection of eggs in her gathered skirt. "Perhaps I'll make cookies."

Pappy grinned. "Now that would be a real treat. I know the men would appreciate it."

"Do you, the men or Rowe prefer any dish?" Not that she could make many, but armed with *Beeton's Book of Household Management*, she felt certain she could tackle most anything. After all, cooking was simply a matter of following directions.

He shrugged. "Long as it's hot and ain't too tough, we're happy."

Pappy's relaxed manner made it easy for her ask more questions. "How long have you and Rowe lived out here?"

"Close to eight years."

"Do you ever miss home? People?"

"I find sagebrush preferable to people."

She stared again at the eggs she'd collected—a dozen by now—and decided to dare another question. "Why is Boone threatening Rowe? Rowe doesn't want me worrying, but if I'm going to be a good wife I need to understand what's happening."

Pappy patted Kate on the back as he studied Jenna for a moment. "Rowe knows Boone from way back."

"How'd they meet?"

"They crossed paths a few years back. Let's say they didn't see eye to eye."

"You're not telling me much."

"All you need to know is that Boone's crazy and mean as a snake. If you ever see him, run. Don't think you can outsmart or handle him, because you can't."

Jenna wasn't sure what to say next, but just then

good-natured hoots and hollers came from the front yard.

The lines on Pappy's face eased and he chuckled. "Sounds like the boys have gotten themselves a stubborn horse. Let's get those eggs in the kitchen and see what's what."

Jenna hurried into the kitchen with Pappy and Kate behind her and deposited her eggs in the sink. They cut through the house and stepped out onto the front porch.

Across the yard, in the center of the corral, a cowhand sat on the ground near a gray horse. Rowe and another cowhand leaned on the split-rail fence, laughing at the man in the dirt.

Even at this distance, Jenna was struck by how different Rowe looked. In his own element, he was relaxed, his hat tipped back on his head, his arms folded casually across his chest. He looked younger, carefree even. Her heart kicked a little faster as she stared at him.

When the man in the corral brushed the dust from his shirt, one of the cowhands shouted, "Come on, Cisco, you gonna let a little horse boss you around?"

Jenna frowned as she shifted her gaze to the downed man. "Should they be laughing? That man could be hurt."

Pappy chuckled. "Don't worry about Cisco, his rear end is as hard as a rock."

Cisco, a wiry man with weathered skin, climbed to his feet, picked up his hat and brushed more dust from his shirt. He didn't look injured, only mad. "Rowe, that mangy animal is mean. She ain't worth the trouble. I say turn her loose. We don't need her that bad."

The mare whinnied, as if she knew she was the topic of discussion. Her head held high, she pranced around the ring, her well-honed body moving with natural grace. A thick mane fringed bright eyes.

Rowe shook his head. "You're giving up too easily. She's a prize."

Cisco planted his hat on his head. "My backside says otherwise."

The other cowhand cackled. Like Cisco, he wore denim, flannel and chaps. His long, lean body was whittled down to muscle and bone—by backbreaking work in the saddle, Jenna surmised. He wore a dirty red kerchief around his neck, a ten-gallon hat and a handlebar mustache.

Pappy pointed to him. "That's Blue. Honest as the day is long and can rope a steer from fifty feet away." Smooth skinned and reed thin, he looked younger than Rowe by a good dozen years. "Not much more than twenty years old, but he's one of the hardest working men I know.''

Jenna studied his scuffed chaps and dusty clothes. "Why do they call him Blue?''

"He grumbles a lot, always seems to be in a foul mood. But he's loyal.''

Rowe pushed away from the fence and strode toward Cisco, his long legs eating up the distance. "Let me show you how it's done.''

Good-naturedly, Blue poked Cisco when he took Rowe's place at the fence. "Don't you think you're getting a little *old* to be breaking wild horses, Rowe?'' he called out. "An old man like you might break a rib. Maybe you'd best give Cisco one more try.''

All the men, including Pappy, laughed as Rowe moved toward the skittish mare that stood on the far side of the corral. She snorted and pawed the dirt with her hoof.

Chuckling, Rowe pulled his hat down, shading his eyes, and strode toward the horse. "Watch and learn, boys.''

"You ain't exactly known for your way with the ladies,'' Cisco called out.

"The ladies at the Golden Beehive sure don't mind him,'' Blue said, his hands cupped around his mouth.

"I hear Honey thinks he's real sweet," Cisco countered.

When Blue spotted Jenna, his grin vanished. He yanked off his hat and swatted Cisco in the chest. "Hush up, there's a lady present," he said in a stage whisper.

The men turned as Jenna and Pappy, with Kate in his arms, reached the fence. The cowboys' smiles dissolved, and a crimson hue colored their faces. Cisco snatched off his hat and puffed out his chest.

Jenna stifled a grin of her own as she stared at the duo. They reminded her of schoolboys who'd just been caught putting a frog in their teacher's desk.

At the mention of her presence, Rowe turned. When he spotted Jenna, the laughter in his eyes faded and was replaced by a look that reminded her of smoldering coals.

Proudly, Pappy hoisted Kate up a little higher. "Boys, I want you to meet the new Mrs. Mercer and her youngun, Miss Kate."

Jenna tore her gaze from Rowe's when Cisco and Blue approached her, hats in hand, staring at her and Kate as if they'd never seen a woman or a baby before.

Blue was the first to speak. "Welcome, ma'am. Blue Malone." He tugged off his work glove, wiped his hand on his dusty shirt and extended it to Jenna. He looked rougher up close, but there was a sincere kindness in his eyes that touched her heart.

Jenna took his hand without hesitation. "The pleasure's mine, Mr. Malone."

Cisco sniggered. "We ain't got no misters out here, ma'am." He held out his ungloved hand. "I'm Cisco Brady. That's just Cisco."

Jenna smiled. "It's good to meet you both." She wanted to make a good impression with her husband's men, but didn't know what type of protocol one followed out here.

Kate broke the silence by gurgling loudly and cooing when she saw Rowe approach the fence. She presented him with a wide, toothless grin. He reached out and chucked her under the chin.

"Morning again, Jenna," Rowe said, his gaze shifting from the child to her.

It was Jenna's turn to blush. "Morning."

Rowe winked at her. "Be back as soon as I tame this horse."

She cocked an eyebrow. "You sound pretty sure of yourself. That horse doesn't look like she trusts you very much."

The cowhands sniggered and turned their faces so Rowe couldn't see their smiles.

Undaunted, Rowe shrugged. "It's my job to show her I can be trusted."

Before she could respond, he turned and started toward the horse once more, moving with confidence.

"You been trying for three seasons to tame that horse and you ain't had no luck so far," Pappy said.

Rowe scooped up the horse's reins from the dust. "This year's going to be different."

Cisco lingered close to Pappy and Kate. He was enchanted by the baby and had started to entertain her with a variety of silly faces. The child laughed, enjoying the attention.

Blue remained beside Jenna, staring at his thumb as if it held the secrets of life. "Mrs. Mercer, about what I said earlier...about the Beehive. It weren't exactly true, I mean about Rowe visiting that place. I mean, that is, he'll make you a fine husband."

Jenna took pity on the man, who was clearly embarrassed about his joke. Still, she couldn't resist teasing him just a little. "I'm afraid I didn't catch much of what you said," she lied. "Perhaps if you'd care to repeat it? I do love a good joke."

He glanced up at her, a mixture of relief and shock on his chiseled features. "Oh, no, ma'am. I mean to say, it weren't very funny at all, Mrs. Mercer."

She bit back a grin. "Call me Jenna. Mrs. Mercer feels too formal out here."

Visibly relaxing, Blue straightened his shoulders. "Thank you, ma'am."

The two turned toward the corral just as Rowe wrapped the reins around his gloved hand and grabbed hold of the saddle's pummel. Quick as a cat, he dug one foot in the dusty stirrup and climbed into the saddle.

The instant Rowe's backside touched the leather saddle, the mare's ears flattened and she started to buck and kick. The men hooted and hollered their encouragement.

Jenna shaded her eyes with her hand, blocking out the midday sun. She drew in a breath, humbled by the strength of the horse, which could easily toss Rowe off and break his neck.

And the mare did her best to do just that. She whinnied and spat as she raced around the ring, kicking up clouds of dust. Rowe's hat flew off, but he held on tight to the reins as the seconds clicked by.

"Show her who is boss!" Blue yelled.

Jenna, the cowboys and even Kate watched silently as Rowe battled the mare. Seconds turned into a minute and then two. The muscles in Rowe's back and arms bunched under his sweat-stained shirt. Finally, the horse's breathing became labored and she grew tired of the fight.

Only when the mare's pace slowed to a trot did Jenna release the breath she'd been holding. Her heart raced, as if she, too, had been engaged in the struggle.

Blue chuckled, pushing his hat back on his head with his index finger. "Well, I never would have believed you could tame that filly after last year."

Jenna turned to Blue. "What happened last year?"

He grinned. "When he tried to break her, she sent him flying. He fell hard, and before he could stand up again, she bit him on the shoulder."

"Pappy wanted to shoot her, but Rowe wouldn't let him," Cisco added.

A thick lather had formed on the horse. Rowe still held on tight as her gait slowed to a walk, but as he rode the horse around the rink, his stance relaxed.

"Looks like that filly might be taking a shine to you, Rowe," Cisco said.

Rowe winked at Jenna. "About time."

At the sound of Rowe's voice, the mare's ears twitched, then flattened against her head. "She doesn't look happy to me," Jenna called out. "Perhaps you've misread her."

Rowe patted the horse on her neck. "Not likely."

Before Jenna could respond, the mare stopped, reared up on her hind legs and sent Rowe reeling backward into the dirt.

Chapter Eight

"Rowe!" Jenna screamed.

Rowe heard the panic in her voice as he struggled to breathe. The fall had knocked the wind from him, stunned him good, and it was taking longer than he'd expected to catch his first breath.

Her skirts grazed his legs and her butter-soft fingertips brushed the hair from his forehead, but he couldn't open his eyes to signal he was okay and that any minute now he'd start breathing.

Chest aching and muscles cramping, he commanded his traitorous lungs to work. His head spun and his pulse rate raced.

"Rowe, please, speak to me," Jenna pleaded.

The heartache in her voice goaded him. He hated the fear he heard. Digging deep, he sucked in that first painful breath. The chilly air clawed its way into his lungs, filling them to capacity. His chest burned, but the influx of oxygen eased the cramping in his body. Gingerly, he took a second breath, then a third, until finally he was able to inhale and exhale normally.

"Thank heavens!" Jenna said.

Her concern touched him. Getting thrown was worth it. He'd have told her so if his head didn't feel like a bull had trampled it.

"Rowe, can you hear me?" Jenna whispered close to his ear. Damn, but she smelled good.

Summoning all his concentration, he pried open his eyelids. Bright sunlight shone behind Jenna, who was little more than a fuzzy figure of lily-white skin and blond curls. He blinked, refocused, and slowly her features grew sharper.

"Jenna," he rasped.

"Yes." Watery blue eyes stared at him. "Are you all right?"

He tried to sit up, but his ribs ached and he knew he'd likely bruised one or two of them. He relaxed back against the dirt. "I'm fine."

"Can you move your feet?" Cisco said. The cowhand stood over him, frowning, his hands resting on his narrow hips.

Rowe moved his legs and his arms. He winced. "They hurt like hell, but they work."

Blue held up two fingers. "How many?"

Rowe squinted. "Two."

Blue's scowl relaxed. "You'll live then, I reckon. But you've got a gash on your head that might need a stitch or two."

Rowe grimaced as he slowly sat up, swayed and steadied himself. Warm blood trickled down his dirt-caked cheek.

"Maybe you better lie back down," Jenna suggested.

Rowe touched his fingertips to his forehead, cursed the bright red on his gloves. "I'm fine."

Jenna brushed the dirt from his cheek. "Are you sure? You don't look well."

The cowhands circled around him. No one said what each knew. Crippling injuries happened even to men like Rowe Mercer. He'd been lucky today.

"Rowe, ain't like you to let a filly best you," Pappy said.

Rowe glanced at the horse standing on the other side of the rink. She eyed him warily, ready to bolt if he approached. "There's a first time for everything."

"I'll turn her loose," Pappy said.

Rowe had taken the horse's surrender for granted, and she'd taken exception. He'd deserved exactly what he'd gotten. "No. She stays."

Cisco hooked his thumbs in his belt. "Mistakes happen when a man's more interested in showing off than doing his job."

Rowe didn't need Cisco or anyone else reminding him he'd been distracted by Jenna. The thousand or so bruises on his body wouldn't let him forget his foolish blunder. He stretched out his arms and flexed his fingers, testing. "My mind was on the job."

"You was riding around like a green wrangler too cocky for his own britches. Luck saved your worthless hide today," Pappy said.

"You worry too much," Rowe said.

Jenna's blue eyes snapped with anger. "That's enough out of all of you. Rowe needs tending, not conversation."

He squeezed her hand reassuringly. "There's no point getting upset."

Jenna arched a slender eyebrow. "No point? I know a bad fall when I see one, Rowe Mercer." Her brittle voice didn't distract him from the way her hands trembled when she shoved back a curl.

"I've had a half-dozen falls worse than this."

"Hard to believe."

"Sorry I scared you, darlin'."

Her pale cheeks coloring, she cleared her throat and focused on his cut. "Hold still while I look at this."

"Kinda bossy, Mrs. Mercer."

"I've a right to be." Pulling a clean, lace-trimmed handkerchief from her pocket, she dabbed it against the cut on his forehead. "It might need a stitch or two."

He stared at the frown on her delicate lips, wanting to taste them again. "I've had stitches before."

"You could've cracked your skull wide-open." She inspected his wound more closely.

"You're cute when you're mad," he whispered.

Her cheeks turned crimson. "I am not!" She pressed his fingers against the bloodied handkerchief. "Hold this, so you don't bleed all over everything."

Complying, he winked at her. "Yes, ma'am."

She dropped her gaze, then turned toward Pappy. "Do you have anything I can use to patch him up?"

Pappy nodded. "Sure do, Mrs. Mercer. Kate and I will fetch it now."

"Good." As Pappy and the baby headed toward the house, she turned to the other men. "Cisco, Blue, help me get him to his feet."

The two cowhands helped Rowe to stand, albeit a little roughly. His ribs still throbbed, but his head and vision had cleared.

Jenna hovered close and wrapped her slender arm around him. He noted the determined concentration furrowing her brow. He liked having her body nestled against his.

He was unreasonably pleased by Jenna's attentions. He could've had Blue patch him up as he'd done a half-dozen times before, but Rowe wasn't ready to surrender his wife yet. Her talk of leaving still lurked in his mind, and he needed to be close to her.

He gave her a little more of his weight, hugging her close. "Maybe I should sit down a spell."

Jenna searched his face for signs of relapse. "Let's get you inside."

Rowe nodded. "You're the boss."

Cisco sniggered. "The boys and me have more experience doctoring cuts and scrapes."

"Jenna can take it from here," Rowe said.

"Maybe we best put Rowe in charge of taming the ponies," Cisco added good-naturedly. "Ain't as far to fall when your feet're dragging on the ground."

Rowe and the other men laughed at the image. The tension broken, they traded a few more jokes and barbs before he realized Jenna wasn't smiling.

She glared at Rowe's men. "Shame on all of you for making light of such a serious matter."

"They're just having some fun, darlin'" Rowe said easily.

Out of respect for Jenna, the cowhands struggled to hide their laugher. They dropped their gazes and kicked the dirt with scuffed boots.

"Sorry, Miz Jenna," Blue offered. "Meant no

disrespect, but we've seen Rowe survive a stampede, a blizzard and a gunshot. A bitsy bump on the head don't seem so bad.''

''Maybe you better take the rest of the day off, Rowe,'' Cisco said. He struggled to keep a straight face.

Winter was coming and there were fences to mend, but the idea of passing the afternoon alone with Jenna in their room overrode good sense. Once she'd patched him up, there was no telling what could happen. A few stolen hours wouldn't hurt. ''I'll see you boys later.''

Cisco and Blue rolled their eyes and choked back their laughter. Jenna didn't say anything as she led him toward the porch.

As Rowe reached for the front door, Blue shouted, ''We'll be right out here if you need us, Rowe.''

''Yea,'' Cisco teased. ''Just give us a shout if you need a helping hand.''

''I've got everything under control,'' Jenna said, a note of steel in her voice.

Rowe let Jenna guide him into the house, through the main room and to the kitchen.

She held on to his arm as he eased his bruised backside onto a chair. ''I'll get something to clean that cut.''

Pappy stood in the doorway, Kate cuddled

against his chest. "I've put clean rags, a needle and thread, water and whiskey on the table. You sure you can handle this?"

"Thank you, Pappy. I've stitched cuts before," Jenna said. "If you would, watch Kate for me? Once I've cleaned Rowe up I'll come for her."

"No rush. The boys is dying to play with her."

With Pappy and Kate gone, Jenna moved to the thick oak table. Her hands were steady as she reached for the pitcher, carefully filled the basin with water and then retrieved the clean cloth, needle and thread.

As Rowe sat on the edge of the chair, he pulled back the handkerchief she'd given him, inspected it to gauge how much he was bleeding, then pressed it back against the wound. "Your first husband teach you how to stitch a cut?"

Jenna's face was rigid, all-business as she threaded the needle. "No, my father."

"He was a doctor, too?"

"A drunk. When he drank too much he often fell. More than once he cut his head. My mother and sister never had the stomach for patching him up, so I learned how."

"I never thought the wealthy worried about the cost of doctors."

"Every fortune has its limits." She laid the threaded needle on the table and dampened the cloth. "Father had a taste for gambling as well as the bottle. When the creditors started cutting us off, money for doctors wasn't there." A bitter edge had crept into her voice.

She removed the soiled handkerchief and reexamined the wound before she wiped away all the blood and dirt around it. "Do you want some whiskey? It'll dull the pain," she said matter-of-factly.

His fisted hands rested on his thighs. "Just do it."

She arched an eyebrow, but didn't argue. Instead, she picked up the needle and stepped between his legs. His thighs brushed her knees and her breasts were at his eye level. He'd have savored having her so near, but all thoughts left his brain when, with a steady hand, she pricked the needle through his torn skin and tugged the suture closed. Rowe held his breath as she put in another stitch, then another.

It took four stitches in all to close the wound, and by the time Jenna cut the thread and tied off the last knot, sweat trickled down his back.

Her face looked a shade paler, but otherwise she was calm. She gently brushed his hair back and studied her handiwork. "You shouldn't have much of a scar. But I imagine you'll have a headache."

With her so close, he barely noticed the pain in his head. Instead his thoughts centered around sliding his hands down her slim waist and cupping her buttocks. "I'm fine."

She dabbed whiskey on another clean cloth and pressed it to his wound. He sucked in his breath through clenched teeth, hissing.

"I'm sorry, but it's the only way to make sure the wound is truly clean," she said.

He waited a beat as the burning eased, then quirked the corner of his mouth. "Pappy would have said I deserved it—for being careless."

Emotion clouded her eyes, and as quickly as a summer storm swept over the plains, tears filled them. She tilted her head back, as if struggling to control the flood. Unable to speak, she concentrated on wiping the dirt off his forehead.

Surprised, he took her hands in his. "What's this about, Jenna?"

She stared at his long fingers wrapped around her wrist. "Nothing. I'm fine. Just a delayed reaction from your mishap."

"Jenna…" he prompted.

Tears slid down her cheeks. She released a ragged sigh. "Two hours ago, I was ready to pack my bags and leave you." She managed a wobbly smile that didn't reach her eyes. "Now, I'm fretting over the thought that I could have lost you. I know I'm being silly. But I've lost so many people.''

''Your husband.'' The words snapped with vinegar. Petty, Rowe knew, but he hated the idea of her pining over *him.*

She dropped her gazed to her hands. ''Yes, Everett of course, but also my sister and my parents. In one way or another, they've all gone from my life forever.''

Rowe took her hands in his and pulled her closer, already regretting his petty thoughts. ''I'm not going anywhere.''

She shook her head. ''You've no control over the future.''

''I refuse to live in fear, and you shouldn't, either.''

She traced her finger around the top button of his shirt, lost in thought. ''You should be more careful.''

He stroked her hair. ''I'm too mean to die.''

She managed a faulty smile. ''You're not mean. Overbearing maybe, but not mean.''

He slid his fingers down her slim waist and rested them on her hips. ''If I'm overbearing, it's because I want to keep you safe. I don't want to lose *you,* Jenna.''

Even tear streaked and smudged with dirt, her

face was so elegant, so fine boned. A nagging feeling in his gut warned she wasn't suited for life out here. But he was too selfish to let her go.

He tugged her forward a step until her breasts nearly touched his chest. She rested her hands on his shoulders, obviously content to be close. Having her this near, wanting her with such fire, consumed him.

He'd promised her a month, yet he'd taken every chance he could to touch her today. The waiting stretched out before him, as endless as the plains.

Perhaps a taste of her could satisfy him. Just a taste.

He reached for her and pressed his lips to hers. She accepted him easily, opening her mouth to him and wrapping her arms around his neck. So soft, so good. Here, now, alone with her as he was, the connection between them felt strong, and he believed everything was possible.

Blood coursed through his body, numbing his aching ribs, blinding him to everything but her. He stroked the inside of her mouth with his tongue, forcing himself to go slow, to savor, when he wanted only to devour.

Deftly, he cupped her breast with his hand, relishing the feel of her. She arched slightly, pushing into his palm. Wanting more, he unfastened the top five buttons of her bodice, exposing the soft white skin. He kissed her creamy breasts through the filmy material of her chemise until her nipples tightened into peaks. A soft mew escaped her lips as she closed her eyes. Her unbridled response filled him with undeniable pleasure.

"Miz Jenna, your gear has arrived from town," Pappy shouted from the main room.

The old-timer's voice startled Jenna. She jumped back and reached for the buttons on her bodice. "I can't believe we were so blatant."

"We're married," Rowe nearly growled in frustration. He wanted to pull her back into his arms, but the moment was shattered, the bond severed. "Pappy's always had bad timing."

Her fingers trembled as she refastened her buttons. "I'd say it's excellent."

Before she could scurry away, Rowe captured her face in his hands and kissed her once more. This time the kiss was feather soft, but it held the promise of more.

He gave her a moment to right her skirt and then, with his hand pressed to the small of her back, he guided her to the front porch. "Let's go see what you've brought."

They discovered a wagon piled with crates and furniture. Blue and Cisco had already tossed back the tarp and unloaded four dainty looking chairs, two richly carved tables and three crates.

Jenna grabbed Rowe's arm. Girlish excitement lit her face. "This is wonderful."

Her unguarded joy bolstered his spirits. "So I see."

Cullum, the stagecoach driver, sauntered up to Rowe and Jenna. He touched the brim of his felt hat. "Mrs. Mercer, my load from Denver was light, so I was able to bring your belongings earlier than expected."

"Thank you so much," Jenna exclaimed. She hugged the driver and hurried to inspect the unloading.

Cullum coughed as his face turned crimson. "You're welcome."

Rowe shoved his hands in his pockets and managed a smile. "She leaves me speechless, too."

Cullum rubbed the back of his neck with his hand. "She's all the folks in town talk about. The ladies in town is planning on paying you a visit in the next few weeks if you don't bring her into town."

"Great."

"They're as curious about her as they were about her furniture."

Rowe groaned. "Just what I need—a bunch of cackling ladies swarming around me."

He studied the collection of furniture and boxes as Jenna stood anxiously by the wagon. Even from this distance, Rowe could see the furniture was fancy, a world apart from the serviceable furnishings in his house, which he'd made out of birch and rawhide.

His unease growing, Rowe wandered over to Jenna. "I knew it was too good to be true."

"What?" Jenna asked, beaming.

"That I'd married a woman who could pack light."

She laughed. "Believe it or not, I sold most of what I had in Alexandria months ago so I could pay my rent."

He hated the idea that she'd been forced to sell her things. "That so?"

"I was able to save my favorite pieces and I'm so glad now. The extra furniture will make our house more comfortable."

Our house. Warmth washed over his heart, once frozen to the possibilities of hearth and home. He stared at her a long moment, drinking in every detail about her. Already Jenna made him want so much more from life. "Yes, it'll make our house comfortable."

Pappy came up to Jenna and handed Kate to her. "The fellows are about to unload a piano."

"It's very heavy," Jenna warned. "It took five men to load it onto the wagon in Alexandria." Kate grinned at the sound of Jenna's voice and laid her head on her shoulder.

"Piano?" Rowe asked as he watched Pappy scurry to the wagon, where his men were pushing the polished upright instrument toward the back.

Jenna hugged the child close. "I know it's an extravagance, but I hated to leave it behind. My grandmother gave it to me and I want Kate to learn how to play."

Music to fill their home. He imagined a Christmas with Jenna at the piano, Kate and his sons surrounding her. "We'll find a corner for it."

Rowe and Cullum went to the wagon and, together with the other men, slid it across the bed of the wagon and then lowered it to the ground. It landed with a hard thump. The hammers bounced against the strings, creating a groaning sound.

Pappy paused to catch his breath. "I sure hope you can play this thing. I'd hate to think I busted my insides for something that's just gonna collect dust."

Jenna grinned. "I passed many happy hours playing that piano."

Rowe handed down a round stool to Pappy. "Then play us a tune, Mrs. Mercer."

"Out here?"

"Why not?"

"Yeah, Miz Jenna," Pappy said, putting the stool in front of the piano. "Play us a tune."

"Very well." Jenna handed Kate to him and took her place in front of the piano. She smoothed her skirts as if she were in a fancy parlor, not a dusty patch of land in the middle of nowhere. She flexed her fingers, then laid them on the ivory keys.

She pressed two or three notes, listening. "The trip has thrown the piano out of tune. Nothing I play will sound exactly right."

"No one cares about that," Rowe said. "Go on, play."

Jenna began to perform a soft, haunting tune that flowed from her as if came from her heart. She closed her eyes, losing herself in the music.

The melody washed over Rowe, transporting him to a world alien to him. In a flash of memory, he remembered two fine ladies in St. Louis long ago, gliding over the boardwalks, their full black skirts swaying gently with each step. They'd passed so close he could smell their lilac perfume, but they'd never noticed him standing in his soiled duster, his hat tipped in respect.

Unsettled by the memory, Rowe forced his thoughts back to the present.

Jenna played for several minutes more before she realized everyone around her had grown silent. She stopped and glanced around, chagrined. "Sorry, I got carried away."

Blue pushed his hat back on his head. "Real fancy."

"High society," Cisco offered.

Jenna moistened her lips as she looked at Rowe. "And you hated it."

Blue shrugged. "Now, it ain't that I hated it exactly, but it weren't to my personal tastes."

"Reminds me of a sour-faced schoolteacher I had once," Cisco said.

Jenna laughed. "What songs do you like?"

Blue hooked his thumbs in his belt and sauntered up to the piano. "Do you know 'The Cowboy's Sweet By and By'?"

She shook her head.

"How about 'The Little Old Shanty on the Claim'?"

"Maybe if you hummed a few bars," she suggested.

"Goes like this." Blue belted out two stanzas.

Jenna listened, then played a few keys on the piano that resembled Blue's tune. Encouraged,

Blue started at the beginning of the song and sang it again. Jenna picked up the melody and played along with him.

The other men joined in. Blue and Cisco hooked arms and started to swing in circles.

Rowe was struck by how easily Jenna had won the hearts of his men. She'd brought light into all their lives.

Yet as he stared at Jenna surrounded by the tables, chairs and rugs suited for Virginia society, he wondered if his uncivilized, hard world would one day extinguish the light in her.

Chapter Nine

An hour later, Jenna gasped at the sound of crystal shattering against stone. She stopped unpacking the crate of books Rowe had just carried in from the wagon, and turned toward the hearth. Pappy knelt by broken shards of a cut-crystal dove figurine. It had been one of a kind, but its real value to Jenna was sentimental.

Now it was gone.

Pappy's gnarled hands hovered over the broken pieces, a deep crimson flush coloring his cheeks. "Oh, Miss Jenna, I am so sorry."

Years of etiquette training helped her mask her disappointment. "It's all right, Pappy," she said.

He shook his head. "No it ain't. It ain't right at all. I should have been more careful." The sorrow in his voice tightened her throat.

Jenna knelt next to him and picked up a jagged

fragment of a wing. "Don't worry about it. I never liked the dove much, anyway," she lied.

Pappy tried to piece together two sections. "It was real fine, I could tell."

She managed a smile. "Please don't give it another thought. It was much too fussy and really doesn't belong here."

"I'm as clumsy as a bull."

Jenna squeezed the old man's hand. "If you don't stop worrying over a worthless piece of glass, I will get angry." In truth, she feared she'd weep.

He sucked in a deep breath. "You're a good woman, Jenna Mercer."

"You give me too much credit. There are more important things in life to worry over than broken glass." She nodded toward the door. "Go on outside. I'll clean up here. I know you've got chores that need doing, and don't have the time to hold my hand while I unpack crates of useless things."

Pappy stared at her a beat longer, as if assuring himself she meant what she'd said. Finally, he shook his head, rose and went outside.

Jenna waited until Pappy left before she let her shoulders slump. She picked up what had been the crystal base and turned it over. The name Victoria etched into the glass jumped out at her. For an instant Jenna couldn't breathe. The loss of her sister and her old life sliced through her heart. Suddenly the sweeping changes that had turned her life upside down seemed too much.

Life had been a whirlwind since Victoria's death. Caring for Kate, her parents' abandonment and her move West had left Jenna no time to grieve. The dove's destruction had cracked the calm facade she'd so carefully maintained, and her emotions bubbled to the surface.

She started to gather up the pieces, thinking that maybe she could fix the figurine. She pressed two sections together. They didn't match. She let out a sigh, fighting tears. Crying over the figurine was foolish, but the tears came nonetheless.

As she gathered the remaining pieces, Rowe strode into the room, a cherry end table in his hands. "Pappy says he broke something?"

She quickly brushed away her tears and sucked in a deep breath. "It's nothing."

Rowe set the table down. She felt him looming over her as she gathered the pieces.

He squatted beside her and frowned at the mess. He picked up a piece and inspected it. Sunlight danced on the shard. "Pappy says it looked valuable."

A dismissive laugh tripped from her. "Please tell Pappy not to give it another thought."

Rowe searched her face as if weighing her

words. She imagined his dark gaze could see past her polite smile right into her heart. The idea unsettled her.

She didn't want anyone else fussing needlessly over her. She stood. "I'd best see if I can find a broom."

He stood. "What's wrong?"

She moved to step around him but he blocked her path. "You're upset about that bird, aren't you?"

"No."

A thick eyebrow arched. "You're a poor liar."

His words struck home. "Honestly, Rowe. Stop looking so serious." She kept her voice deliberately light. "I'm fine."

He muttered an oath. "If you're upset about that," he said, nodding to the broken dove, "I'll have it fixed."

"No, please don't do that. I told Pappy I didn't care."

"You do care."

"No, I don't," she said with more force.

She wanted to lean into him, needed him to wrap her arms around him. It had been so long since anything had felt right, and she needed him to tell her everything was okay—that she'd be fine.

But deep emotions weren't part of their bargain. Yes, the sexual attraction between them was strong. She trusted him with her safety, her security. But feelings were a different matter. How could she expect Rowe, a man who was a stranger to her in so many ways, to understand what the loss of the dove meant?

She swallowed. "You must have work to do."

"It'll keep."

She tried to pull her hand free of his, but he wouldn't release her.

"When's the last time you ate?"

"I had coffee and a biscuit this morning."

"That's all? No wonder you're pale." He nodded toward the kitchen table. "Sit down."

"You don't need to worry."

"Someone should fuss over you." He pushed her into a chair and strode toward the cupboard.

He took a plate from the shelf and loaded it with biscuits and slices of ham from the larder. He set the plate in front of her. "Eat."

To humor him, she nibbled a piece of ham and was surprised it tasted so good. "Thanks."

"You're not by yourself anymore."

"I know."

He looked at her with such intensity it made her dizzy. "Do you?"

She squirmed a bit. "Yes, of course."

"Then why are you holding out on me?" He

poured water into a tin cup and put it in front of her, then took the seat next to her.

Jenna blinked, his directness making it difficult to string two thoughts together. "I—I'm not." She raised her chin a fraction, determined to disprove the truth. "Ask me anything."

His eyes narrowed a fraction. "First you eat."

As she ate one bite and then another, she expected him to fire questions at her. Instead, he waited until she'd eaten half the food on her plate. "Why were you so upset about the bird?"

"I wasn't upset about…" She stopped, sighed. "It was a gift from my father to my mother to mark the birth of my younger sister."

"Where is she now?"

"She's dead."

"I'm sorry," he said softly.

Unable to speak for fear her voice would tremble, Jenna sank into an awkward silence.

"How long has it been?"

"Less than a year."

"How?"

A shudder passed through her. "It's a long story."

He folded his arms over his chest. "I've got time."

"It's the past." She felt weary, drained now. "Thank you for the meal."

"What aren't you telling me?"

"There's nothing to tell."

"Tell me about Victoria."

Jenna let her mind drift back to memories she'd worked hard to forget. She spoke carefully, as if treading near the lip of a cliff. "Everyone loved Victoria. She was so beautiful."

"As beautiful as you?"

Jenna laughed. "I'm not beautiful. Victoria *was* beautiful."

Rowe scowled. "You're wrong. You are beautiful."

"You never saw Victoria."

"I don't have to. Tell me more."

Jenna pinched a piece of biscuit but didn't eat it. "My parents pampered her almost from the day she was born. They knew she would grow into a beauty and would someday make a fine match."

He grunted. "You talk about her as if she were a horse."

"Oh, no. My parents loved Victoria. They only wanted the best for her. She would have married one of the wealthiest men in Virginia if she hadn't—" The word hung in Jenna's throat, twisting her insides.

As if he'd sensed her hesitation, he shifted the conversation away from Victoria. "What plans did your parents have for you?"

"What do you mean?"

"They wanted you to marry well."

"Well, yes, I suppose. It was never discussed, really. Victoria was their priority."

"Did they approve of our marriage?" His eyes possessed a keenness that made her uncomfortable.

"I wrote and told them of my plans to marry you, but we made our final arrangements so quickly I left Alexandria before they could respond."

His jaw tightened a fraction. "What about your first marriage?"

She couldn't bring herself to lie outright. She rose and turned toward the window, staring out at the bold, jutting mountains in the distance. "I don't think they ever gave Everett much thought."

He rose, moved behind her. "Why not?"

"Victoria's social obligations consumed all their time. There were many parties for her. We had limited resources and not enough capital to sponsor two daughters. I understood that they had to choose."

He grunted. "What did they know of Everett?"

"They'd only met him once or twice, but they'd heard good things about him, plus his family was well connected. Connections have always been very important to my parents."

"When Kate marries I will know all there is to

know about her intended, and I don't give a damn about family connections."

Rowe's gruff paternalism touching her heart. Her own father had been distant, too busy with his gambling and social ambitions to care whom she'd chosen. "Family means a lot to you."

"Yes."

"Did you come from a large one?" The question reminded her again that they were strangers in so many ways.

"No." He shrugged. "Been on my own so long I can't say I know what it feels like to miss anyone."

"Take it from me, it feels awful."

Something flickered in his gaze as he stared at her. "We're not just talking about your sister."

"I miss what was familiar, what I understood. I knew what to say and do in Virginia. But I don't miss the people, not even Everett, really." She brushed a curl from her face. "It's as if I woke up one morning understanding all the rules, what was expected of me. And then in the blink of an eye the rules changed and I'm living a life with a whole different set of expectations I don't fully understand yet."

His gaze was clear and direct. "You will find your footing soon enough. You're going to be glad you moved out here," he said with conviction.

His calm faith made her believe everything was going to be fine. "I hope I'm not a disappointment to you."

"You're more than I ever hoped for, Jenna Mercer." His voice was hoarse, thick with an emotion she didn't quite understand.

He leaned closer. His scent, a mixture of fresh air and his own musk, comforted and disturbed her. His face hovered only inches from hers and she noted the subtle shades in his eyes, when before they'd seemed only gray. Her gaze drifted to the thick bramble of his hair, tied neatly at the base of his neck, and then to the scar that trailed along his cheek.

She touched the tip of the scar by his right eye, which began just below the cut she'd just sewed up. "So many scars."

Silent, he didn't pull away, giving her the courage to trail her finger down the pink ridge to the corner of his mouth. "I thought you were a pirate when I first met you."

"I've been called worse."

"How did you get it?"

He captured her hand and turned it over until her palm faced up. "A rustler." He traced circles on her small calluses. "We got into a fight. He pulled a knife."

"What happened to him?" she whispered.

"I killed him." He searched her face, as if looking for signs of fear, but she was determined to hear him out, and held his gaze. "The man I killed was Boone's older brother, Jimmy. I trailed them for days, and when I caught up to them Jimmy pulled a knife. We struggled. I was cut. He was killed. Boone saw it all happen." There was no satisfaction or regret in Rowe's eyes. "Boone was convicted of rustling and sentenced to ten years in prison, but he swore he'd come after me."

"Is that why he was here this morning?"

A bitter smile twisted the corner of his mouth. "He's looking for revenge."

"But he was stealing."

"That doesn't matter to him. What matters is that I killed his brother."

"Who tried to kill you," she insisted.

"Boone and men like him aren't bound by honor. They take what they want because they can. They strike when one of their own is wronged because they like inflicting pain more than retribution."

Cold fear gripped her heart. "Boone's coming after you."

Rowe tensed. "I can handle Boone. He's not going to hurt you or Kate." Steel threaded his words.

She knew deep in her bones that Rowe would

protect Kate and her with his life, if need be. But who would look after him?

"I don't want anything to happen to you." Jenna spoke with more emotion than she'd intended. Her words seemed to strike a chord in him, and his eyes softened. The rough warrior's armor dropped away and she glimpsed vulnerability in his eyes. It nearly stole her breath.

She took his face in her hands. Shocked by the boldness of her thoughts, she couldn't stop the rush of heat that flooded her face or the memory of the kiss they'd shared earlier. Her mouth went dry with wanting.

Rowe smiled. It was a dark, dangerous smile that made her weak with desire. She knew she was tampering with Pandora's box, but she couldn't step away.

She leaned forward, just a fraction. Needing no further invitation, he pulled her into his arms and pressed his lips to hers. This kiss was smoldering, demanding, hot—every bit as good as their last one.

She wrapped her arms round his neck, molding her breasts to his hard chest. His rich male taste tantalized her senses, making her forget everything about the past and the future. In his arms there was only now.

A sensual moan bubbled inside her. Rowe tightened his grip, clutching her hair in his fist. His tongue plunged into her mouth, caressing her, awakening her.

Her knees went weak. The deep drumbeat of desire pounded in her blood, banishing well-laid plans to go slow.

A rough growl, more animal than human, rumbled in Rowe's chest. But when she thought he'd sweep her up into his arms, he pushed away from her.

His mouth was tight, still moist from their kiss, and his eyes looked a bit wild. "I've got to go."

She could only stare at him. Already, without his touch, she felt cold. "What?"

"I've got to leave," he said. "I've a new house to build for us."

Stung, she folded her arms and backed away a step. "Now? But it's the middle of the afternoon. You've only a few hours of daylight left."

Sensing her hurt, he advanced again, held out his hand, then shoved it back in his pockets. "If I don't go now, Mrs. Mercer, I won't be waiting twenty-nine days to make this marriage real."

"But—"

He ran shaky fingers through his thick mane. "I want more than your body, Jenna." His voice was tight, as if speaking was difficult. "I want your trust. And for that, I must keep my promise to you, even if it means waiting.''

Boone stretched out his long legs near the campfire and stared into the flames that snapped and danced in the air. The five men he'd hooked up with slept on their bedrolls nearby. Their breathing was deep and labored, thanks to six bottles of rotgut. He knew none of the men would stir before morning.

Boone was careful not to drink when he had a job to do. His brother, Jimmy, had always said to stay sharp. Drunks, he'd say, landed in jail.

So Boone was doing everything Jimmy would have wanted him to do. ''I'm staying alert, Jimmy, just like you always said.''

Jimmy had always known what to do. Since they was kids, he'd been the planner, the thinker loaded with a gutful of ideas and plans. Boone had been content to rustle cattle here and there, but not Jimmy. He thought big.

Jimmy was the one who first talked of robbing banks. Jimmy was the one who could waltz into a bank as bold as you please and poke his gun through the teller's barred window. Grinning like a cat, he was never in a rush, always enjoying the tension, the smell of fear, the way the teller's hand shook when he shoved the money in a bag.

There'd been a time in Texas when they'd barely escaped a lynch mob. His brother had enjoyed the chase that day, the thrill of outsmarting the law, whereas Boone still got sick when he thought back on it.

He poked a stick into the flames, churning the embers until sparks popped and danced in the air like fireflies.

Jimmy gave Boone courage. Life made sense when Jimmy had been alive.

The day Mercer put a knife in Jimmy, life had become a jumbled mess. Hell, Boone could have stomached the ten years in prison if he'd known Jimmy had been waiting for him. But Jimmy was six feet under in an unmarked grave.

When Mercer had killed Jimmy he'd stolen Boone's life, too.

"It weren't right or fair," he grumbled.

Boone's mind drifted back to yesterday, when he'd ridden onto Mercer's property. He'd not expected much to come of the meeting until he'd seen her.

Jenna Mercer.

A man could live a lifetime without ever coming face-to-face with a woman like that. She had breeding, culture—just the kind of woman Jimmy liked.

Mercer liked her, too. Boone could tell.

The way Boone figured it, Mercer owed him.

A life for a life.

A family for a family.

Mercer had taken the one person in the world that Boone had cared about.

And soon it would be his turn.

Chapter Ten

The weather turned cold over the next two weeks. Rowe and his men split their days between rounding up the calves and framing the new house. All the men expected a harsh winter, and Rowe was determined to have the calves weaned and the roof up on the new house before the first snowfall.

Jenna saw little of him. He rose before dawn and didn't return until after she'd fallen asleep. She had vague recollections of nestling close to him at night, but during the day the rare "yes" or "no" was all they exchanged.

Jenna missed Rowe and how her pulse tripped each time he touched her. But the time alone had allowed her to get to know her new home—and fashion herself into the perfect wife.

Her books made homemaking sound easy, but becoming the perfect wife was tougher than she'd

first thought. The cookstove had an annoying habit
of burning her biscuits, the chickens pecked her
hands each time she gathered eggs without Pappy
at her side, and yesterday the rooster had chased
her around the barn until finally she'd flung her
basket of eggs at the creature. The eggs had shattered in the dirt around the bird, but he had at last
retreated.

Jenna had refused to admit defeat, had bottled
up her fear of failure and swallowed frustrated
tears. Over and over she reminded herself that she
would succeed.

The bright spot in the string of failures was that
Kate was flourishing in the fresh mountain air. Her
cheeks had taken on a rosy hue and she could sit
up on her own now, gurgling happily when Pappy
or one of the other cowhands picked her up. Soon
she'd be crawling.

The babe lay next to Jenna now, playing with
her toes in the center of the massive bed. Jenna sat
cross-legged on the coverlet with her copy of *Beeton's Book of Household Management*. It was
opened to "Duties of the Laundry Maid."

"How hard can it be?" Jenna said to Kate. The
baby cooed and blew a bubble. "You're right, I've
said that before." She nuzzled her face in the
baby's stomach, laughing when the child grabbed

a fistful of her hair. "But I'm not giving up, Katie-bug. I'm going to make our new life work."

She gently pried the baby's hands free, then scanned the book one last time before she snapped it closed. Laundry was going to be easy.

With the book tucked under one arm, she eased off the bed. Her strained muscles ached from beating rugs and carrying pots of water, and she moved with deliberate slowness. She lifted the baby, wincing when her lower back pinched. Her monthly would arrive in the next few days, and she felt sluggish and tired.

Shrugging off her fatigue, she headed outside behind the house, where yesterday she had set up three laundry tubs and a cauldron. She plucked at the clothesline, testing its strength, and peered into the tub filled with freshly mended clothes that had been soaking since last night. Pappy had started a fire for her under the large cauldron earlier this morning. Steam already rose from the warming water.

Jenna laid the baby on a blanket away from the fire, with spoons and a bowl to entertain her. "Watch and learn, Kate. This shouldn't take more than an hour, two at the most."

Four hours later, Jenna's arms hurt and a dull headache throbbed above her left eye as she stirred the clothes around in the hot water. Sweat trickled from her forehead, curling the wisps of hair around her face into ringlets. She wanted to cry.

Trouble had commenced when the fire under the cauldron went out. It took thirty minutes to relight, and when the flames had finally started to crack and pop, Kate began to cry. It took another half hour to feed and change the babe, who decided she'd have nothing to do with her morning nap. So, with the baby on her hip, Jenna fished the clothes out of the soaking tub and dropped them into the hot, soapy water. Mercifully, Kate finally drifted off to sleep in her basket, leaving Jenna with the daunting task of removing the clothes from the boiling water and scrubbing them on the washboard.

Her cheeks flushed, Jenna dug out the first garment with a large wooden paddle. The waterlogged work shirt was heavy and awkward. Boiling water splashed onto her skin. She hissed in through her teeth, refusing to release the paddle. "I can do this. I can do this."

She dropped the shirt in an empty tub equipped with a washboard, touched the scalding fabric and immediately snatched back her hand.

Jenna sat on her haunches and brushed her hair out of her eyes with the heel of her sore hand. Tears of frustration stung her throat.

What had she been thinking? *Easy* and *laundry* didn't belong in the same sentence. "An invention of the devil," she muttered.

But Colorado was where she and Kate belonged, and she was determined to prove herself. Gritting her teeth, she took hold of the fabric and scrubbed it against the washboard, scraping her knuckles in the process. "Damn it."

Cursing made her feel better. So she swore again and again as she dropped the shirt in the soaking tub, now refilled with clean water.

"One down. Thirty-two to go."

It took another forty minutes to do three more shirts, and by the time she lifted her fifth shirt out of the water, she'd decided the laundry nightmare would never end.

The sound of footsteps coming around the house broke her string of muttered oaths. She looked up, hoping it was Rowe. Pride be damned, she needed help.

But it wasn't Rowe. It was Laura Holt.

"Good afternoon, Mrs. Holt!" Jenna said, her tone a bit desperate.

The plump, smiling woman strode across the yard, her lemon-colored skirts billowing in the breeze. She carried a large wicker basket covered with a red-and-white checkered cloth. "Hello,

Jenna! I'd have been out here sooner, but was a bit under the weather.''

"I do hope you're feeling better." She'd never been happier to see anyone in her life. She let the shirt slip off the paddle into the cauldron, uncaring that water splattered on her already damp skirt.

"Fit as a fiddle."

"I'm glad to hear it, Mrs. Holt."

Laura's smile softened with sympathy as her gaze surveyed Jenna's wet skirts, muddied shoes and chaffed hands. "Call me, Laura," she said. She laid her crocheted shawl on a stump, set the basket nearby and rolled up her bright yellow calico sleeves. "Looks like you've got your hands full."

Jenna's shoulders slumped. "I'll never look at grease or dirt the same way again."

Laura chuckled as she inspected the water. "Laundry has a way of tempting the patience of any woman. What most men don't realize is that it's as backbreaking as mending fences or branding. But unlike a brand or a fence, clean laundry doesn't stay clean long. Before you know it, it's time to tackle the chore again."

Jenna grinned. "At the rate I'm going, I won't be done until next week."

Laura took the wooden paddle, plucked out a shirt and dropped it into the washbasin in one smooth move. "With the two of us working we'll have it done before sunset."

Awed, Jenna watched Laura scrub the shirt and plop it in the clear water. "How'd you do that so fast?"

"Lots of practice."

Jenna sighed. "I'm so glad you came."

"Thought it was time to pay you a visit." She nodded to the basket. "Also, I brought a welcome supper."

Jenna drew in a deep breath. "It smells delicious. I hope you'll help me eat it?"

Laura chuckled. "Be pleased to."

Jenna searched for signs of Matt. Finding none, she said, "Don't tell me you came here alone."

Laura removed another garment and dropped it in the washbasin. "Lately, Matt doesn't want me traveling alone. He's worried about the weather, stampedes, you name it. I can shoot as well as any man, but he won't even discuss it." She nodded toward the small rise. "I left Matt and the wagon near the new house. He's helping Rowe and the boys with the roofing."

Jenna knelt in front of the washboard. "I should be offering you tea, not putting you to work."

"Nonsense. I'm here to help as much as visit."

"Thank heavens you came."

Laura's expression grew concerned. "How are you adjusting to ranch life?"

Jenna blew a curl off her forehead. Her skin itched from the lye soap. "Not so good. The housekeeping guide I've read makes homemaking sound so easy. Of course, it assumes I have servants to direct to do the heavy work."

"The work's backbreaking, no doubt about it."

"I had no idea." She started to scrub a shirt on the washboard. "I've a mind to send a note to my mother's laundress and apologize for all the times I wore a dress once and tossed it in the laundry bin."

Laura stared at Jenna's raw, chapped hands. "I don't mean to pry, but how did you end up in Colorado? I mean, this ain't the kind of life a society woman chooses all that often."

"I wanted a fresh start," Jenna said honestly.

"I reckon losing a husband makes a woman want to get away from painful memories."

Jenna kept her gaze on the shirt. "I don't think about the past anymore."

Laura nodded. "You've come to the right place. Today's what counts out here, not yesterday."

Together, the women made quick work of the remaining laundry. In no time, Jenna was pinning the last shirt to the clothesline. "To think I'll be doing this again next week."

Laura wiped her hands on a dry cloth. "There's a woman in town, Mrs. Baxter, who takes in wash. Very reasonable. You should pay her a visit the next time you're in Saddler Creek."

"I guess I need to prove to myself that I can do it," Jenna replied.

"I used to do everything myself, didn't take help from anybody. Then I had a miscarriage last spring. Since then I don't worry so much about doing everything perfectly."

Jenna heard the sadness in Laura's voice and wanted to say something, but she'd learned that words, no matter how sweet, never softened loss. "Join me inside for biscuits and tea. The biscuits are overcooked a little, but they're not that bad."

Laura smiled. "I'd like that. It's been so long since I had a chance to visit with another woman. It gets lonely out here at times."

"Kate should be awake soon. I know she'll enjoy seeing you."

Laura's face brightened. "I can't wait to play with the baby." A sly smile touched her lips. "Can you keep a secret, Jenna?"

"Oh, yes."

"I'm almost completely sure, but I wanted to wait a few more weeks before I tell Matt." She glanced around, making certain no one could overhear. "I'm pregnant. Likely due in late spring."

Jenna clasped Laura's hands in hers. "That's wonderful!"

Laura squeezed Jenna's fingers. "I'm so excited, and I can't tell you what a relief it is to have you here."

"I'll help any way I can."

Laura hooked her arm in Jenna's. "You can start by telling me what it is like giving birth."

A half hour later, the last rays of sunlight hovered above the horizon. Rowe and Matt Holt stood on the hill watching the two women through the kitchen window. Laura was playing with the baby and Jenna was setting the table.

Matt's eyes softened when he saw his wife lift Kate high. "I wasn't sure coming here today was such a good idea. It's only been six months since Laura lost the baby, and I was afraid seeing Kate would upset her. But now I'm glad we came."

Rowe nodded, remembering the night Laura had miscarried. She'd been six months along, and then for no reason had gone into labor. She'd nearly bled to death before the nightmare was over. "The color's back in her cheeks and she's smiling again."

Matt nodded. "It's good to have my wife back." Feminine laughter trailed up the hill. "Looks like the womenfolk have hit it off."

Rowe let out a sigh. "I'm glad. This is a lonely life for a woman."

Guilt tugged at his conscience. He'd purposefully kept clear of Jenna these last two weeks. He made sure one of his men was close by, standing guard, and he'd even stolen peeks at her, but he'd been careful to keep his distance. Since the moment he'd kissed her in the kitchen, he'd known that if he didn't stay away, he'd make love to her. And it had been important that he honor his word to Jenna.

He'd meant what he'd said when he told her he wanted her trust. "Any more signs of Boone?"

"Just what I told you last week. Rode near the ranch, made sure I saw him, but didn't do anything," Matt answered.

"It's a matter of time."

"He might not have the gumption to try anything without his brother."

"Don't count on it. The bastard's crazy, which means logic doesn't enter into his decisions."

A solemn silence hovered before Matt said, "How's Jenna managing?"

Rowe released another sigh. "Let's say she's got heart."

"Which means she doesn't know the first thing about ranching."

"Not the first thing."

Matt laughed. "Many grooms have suffered at the hands of well-meaning brides. Laura and I were having a laugh this morning about some of the meals she made when we were first married. She burned a steak so bad once it snapped clean in half."

"If Jenna becomes half the cook Laura is, I'll be grateful."

Damp laundry flapped in the breeze as they reached the back door. They were greeted by the smell of chicken and pie warming in the oven.

Matt grinned. "Did I mention that Laura packed dinner?"

The taste of the burned biscuit he'd tried to eat this morning still lingered. "You're a saint."

Matt laughed and clamped his hand on Rowe's shoulder. "Let's have supper with our wives."

Our wives. Rowe wondered when a man got used to hearing *wife* associated with his name. He imagined, as with all things, that men and women gradually become accustomed to each other, grew familiar with the other's habits, likes and dislikes. He looked forward to the day when he and Jenna shared the quiet intimacy Matt and Laura had.

Rowe and Matt found the women in the kitchen. A mason jar filled with the last of the season's wildflowers decorated the table, set with four place settings of Jenna's fancy, rose-trimmed china. Silverware glowed in the lantern light.

In the center of the table, Laura's fried chicken overflowed a white platter set next to a heaping bowl of her greens and corn bread. Two cherry pies warmed on the stovetop, next to a small plate of Jenna's very brown biscuits.

Laura sat in one of the sturdy chairs with Kate balanced on her knees. She made faces at the child while the women chatted. The baby cooed.

Rowe pulled off his hat. "Evening, ladies."

Jenna's gaze lifted and touched his. For a heartbeat the two stared at each other. A stray curl brushed the middle of her forehead and her cheeks flushed. She'd grown thinner these last two weeks and she looked exhausted. "Evening."

Later, when they were alone, he would ask her to slow down. "Evening."

"Something sure smells good," Matt said.

Enthralled with the baby, Laura laughed and bounced her up and down. "Matt, come and meet Miss Kate. She's just about the prettiest child I ever did see."

Sorrow washed across Matt's face before he grinned and sauntered over to his wife. He chucked the baby under the chin. "Rowe, I believe you're gonna have to keep your shotgun well oiled when this little gal goes courting. Every young buck in the county will be sniffing.''

Rowe tore his gaze from Jenna. "She's never going to court."

Laura laughed. "Honestly, Rowe, you can't keep Kate from marrying."

"Maybe not, but I'll put any whelp that comes courting through his paces."

The child had his heart. Each morning, hours before sunrise, she'd awaken when he did. Because he'd not had the heart to wake Jenna that first morning, he'd gotten into the habit of giving the baby a morning bottle.

"Woe to the young lad who dares win the hand of Lady Kate." Mock concern filled Matt's voice.

Smiling, Jenna placed her plate of dried biscuits next to Laura's plump pieces of chicken. "Matt, you make Rowe sound like the castle ogre."

"Anything I can do to help?" Rowe asked.

"Just wash up," Jenna said. "Laura's brought all the food and the table's set."

Rowe and Matt scrubbed their hands outside by the pump and within minutes sat at the table. Laura was settled in her chair with Kate nestled on her lap.

Jenna reached for the baby. "Let me take her. If you hold on to her, you won't remember what you ate."

Laura shook her head, grinning. "I'm not ready to give her up. You eat first, then we'll swap."

Jenna let her arms drop. "Are you sure? I've had a lot of practice holding her while managing a plate in the other."

"I'm very sure. Sit. Eat. Kate and I will be fine."

"Kate looks happy in Laura's lap," Rowe said. "Take advantage of her offer and enjoy this good meal."

Jenna's smile waned as she sat. "Okay."

Matt tucked one of Jenna's fine white linen napkins in his shirt collar. "Laura, you've outdone yourself again."

Rowe dropped two pieces of chicken on his plate, along with a heaping spoonful of greens and a large piece of corn bread. "Your chicken is the best in the county. And I can't wait to taste that pie."

Jenna took a piece of chicken and one of her biscuits. With her knife and fork, she cut a ladylike portion of chicken and ate it. "It's delicious."

"Laura can give you the recipe if you like, Jenna," Matt said, his mouth full.

Jenna pried apart her biscuit and spread a generous portion of butter on it. "I'd like that."

"Make sure you learn how to make that pie, too," Rowe said.

"Of course," Jenna murmured. She sighed as she stared at her plate of untouched biscuits.

Rowe noticed that Jenna had grown quiet. She was tired, he supposed, from the work.

Laura glanced from Matt to Rowe as if suddenly annoyed. Cradling the baby with one hand, she took one of Jenna's biscuits with the other. "Jenna, you set a lovely table. I don't think I've ever seen china so fine."

Jenna swallowed the dry biscuit, then chased it down with water. "It doesn't take much talent to arrange a table."

"Nonsense, I wouldn't know where to start. Rowe, you should see all the laundry Jenna managed today. She's a hard worker," Laura continued.

A tug of conscience cooled Rowe's appetite. "She's working too hard as it is." He captured her hand and turned it over. The once smooth palms were red and chafed. "Maybe you should ease up."

She slid her fingers from his, curling them into a fist at her side. "I don't work any harder than any other ranch wife."

He knew ranch life took its toll on men and especially women, but he'd wanted to spare Jenna from as much of it as possible. "Send the laundry to Mrs. Baxter."

She pursed her lips as if he'd said something that offended her. "It's a wife's job—my job—to do the laundry."

"My ranch turns a fine profit, Jenna," he said matter-of-factly. "It's foolish for you to ruin your hands with hot water and lye. Besides, you look exhausted."

She frowned. "I insist on doing my share, Rowe."

Her mood had soured, but for the life of him he couldn't figure out why. "You do a lot," he rushed to say.

Her fork clanged against her plate when she set it down. "Not enough."

"It's not worth arguing over, Jenna. Send the laundry into town. And we'll see about getting you more help out here. Maybe a cook."

"No! Taking care of this ranch is my job. And I'll do the blasted laundry even if it kills me."

Laura and Matt stopped cooing at the baby. They stared at each other, sharing a secret signal.

Laura rose. "Do you mind if Matt and I sneak out early this evening? We really need to get home to tend the stock."

Matt, spotting the glint in his wife's eyes, tossed his napkin by his plate. "Laura's right. Got horses to water."

Jenna accepted the baby from Laura. "Don't leave. I didn't mean to chase you off."

"You need time to yourselves," Laura said reasonably. She gave the baby one last pat. "We'll visit again real soon."

Standing, Jenna looked stricken. "This is my fault."

Rowe stood in turn, still not sure what was wrong. Any woman in her right mind would avoid laundry and chores.

Laura squeezed Jenna's hand. "Nonsense. I'll be back in a couple of days."

Matt grabbed a piece of corn bread. "Got to be going."

Laura reached for her shawl and bonnet. "I'll be by to get the basket in a day or two."

Rowe walked Matt outside and helped him hitch the wagon. "What the hell happened in there?"

Matt groaned, then in a low voice said, "Never have been able to figure out what goes on in Laura's mind, but I got sense enough to know when I'm in trouble."

"You mean *I'm* in trouble?"

"Oh, yeah."

Laura came out then, and Matt helped her into the wagon and bade Rowe good-night. When their buckboard had dipped down over the rise, Rowe turned to find Jenna holding Kate in the doorway.

He started toward her, determined to clear the air between them, but she turned and hurried away.

Rowe shoved a hand through his hair. If he weren't such a ham-fisted cattleman, he'd know what to say to Jenna.

He found her sitting next to the hearth in the living room, near the cradle, where the baby lay. Jenna's face was turned away from him.

"Jenna."

She shook her head. "I'm sorry they left. I drove them away."

He moved closer to her, not sure what she needed from him. "It was time they got home."

"No, it was me. I was a shrew." She looked up at him, tears brimming in her eyes. "I have a habit of disappointing people." The words seemed wrenched from her chest.

"*I'm* not disappointed," he stated.

"Yes, you are! I've botched every task I've tackled since I arrived."

"Ranching is a skill that takes practice. Give it time."

"How much time?"

He stabbed his fingers through his hair. "I don't know."

"How long did it take you to learn ranching?"

He shrugged. "It was different with me. I'm not from the city. I'm used to horses and hard work."

Her eyes grew a little wild. "And I'm not?"

Feeling clumsy, he struggled to find the right words. "What do you want me to say? That you're the perfect wife? You're not. No one is. It's a fact of life."

He realized his blunder then. Her face crumpled as tears streamed down her face. She scooped up the baby, turned on her heel and stormed into the bedroom, slamming the door behind her.

Rowe strode after her, reaching for the doorknob.

"Don't you dare come in here!" she wailed.

Frustrated, he leaned his head against the closed door. "Jenna, what's wrong?"

"If you don't know, then I'm not going to tell you."

"Jenna..." he repeated, his voice sterner.

"Go away!"

Rowe raised his hands in surrender and backed away. When had he lost control of his life?

Chapter Eleven

Rowe didn't come home all night.

Who could blame him? Jenna wondered miserably the next morning. She stood on a hilltop above the ranch and hurled a dried biscuit at a large rock. It whacked against the stone, not even having the decency to crumble before dropping into the dirt like a lead cannonball.

Her calico skirts rippled in the wind. Crisp blue sky touched the mountains that ringed the grassy valley.

From where she stood she had a clear view of the rustic cabin she shared with Rowe, and the two-story, frame house he was working on so furiously. The banging of hammers echoed up the hillside.

Rowe was there, she realized with relief and sorrow. Likely he'd spent last night in the new house.

She hurled another biscuit at the tree, this time missing it completely.

She'd risen before dawn this morning. After she'd bathed and fed Kate, she'd folded the clean laundry, but had found little satisfaction in the crisp stacks of clothes. Frustrated and restless, she'd put Kate down for her afternoon nap, asked Pappy to watch the babe, then scraped the day-old biscuits into the slop bucket and set off to this quiet spot.

Jenna picked up another biscuit and hefted it like a rock as she eyed the half-dozen flour marks on the tree's sun-baked bark.

Dinner with the Holts had been a miserable failure. The food Laura had brought was delicious, far superior to the burned, dried-up fare Jenna had served Rowe these last weeks. No wonder the man had looked as if he was ready to weep when he'd bitten into that first bite of moist chicken. Perhaps if Jenna hadn't felt so lacking, or been so tired, she wouldn't have overreacted to Rowe's suggestions.

She sighed and pressed her fingers to her temple. She had two options: she could keep throwing overcooked biscuits at the tree and continue feeling sorry for herself, or she could find Rowe and apologize.

Her cheeks burned with embarrassment at the

way she'd acted like a spoiled child. She had to find him.

A wind kicked up, rustling the leaves overhead and the grass around her. Goaded into action, she retrieved the bucket and biscuits, set them by the tree and went down the hill to find Rowe.

She'd not seen the new house since she'd arrived, and despite her foul humor was curious. The sounds of a hammer striking nails grew louder as she crossed the grassy clearing.

The frame house was five times the size of the cabin and filled with windows both upstairs and down. A wide porch graced the front. Marveling at the workmanship, Jenna lifted her skirts, climbed the three steps and crossed the wide veranda through the open front door. Daylight streamed through glass windows, casting a cheery glow on the large main room, which was divided into quarters by four unfinished walls. A central staircase, still without a banister, joined the two stories.

At the far end of the first floor, Jenna could make out what was to be a large kitchen. The space adjacent had the look of a dining room. The two front rooms looked as if they could serve as parlor and library.

She touched an unfinished wall, humbled that Rowe had built this for them. Her throat tightened with emotion. No one had ever gone to this kind of trouble for her before.

The hammering stopped and she heard the steady thud of footsteps. She backed toward the front door, suddenly feeling like an interloper.

Rowe appeared at the top of the stairs. He stood shirtless, a hammer clutched in his right hand, and his loose hair, dark as Satan's, brushed his tanned shoulders. With the thick blanket of stubble on his chin, he had the look of a desperado.

The fidgety energy that had plagued her these last few weeks sprang to life, and Jenna wished she hadn't come. "If I'm interrupting your work, I'll go."

"Stay." His deep voice reverberated in the empty house. Tossing down the hammer, he reached for a gray shirt that hung on a nail, pulled it over his head and tucked it into his pants before he strode down the stairs.

His masculine scent blended with the new-wood smell and permeated the space around them. A fine sheen of sweat glistened on his forehead, and a thick mat of hair peeked out of the V created by the unfastened top buttons of his shirt.

Sparks jumped between them. The air seemed as dry as tinder after a long drought. But somehow, Jenna managed not to turn on her heel and run. "I came to apologize for last night."

"No problem." His gruff voice grated like sand-paper.

She moistened her lips. "I normally am not a childish shrew."

"I know."

Her gaze rose to his gray eyes. The intensity in them nearly took her breath away. She didn't see anger reflected in their depths, but something infinitely more unsettling.

Rowe shoved his hands in his pockets. "I didn't say the right things to you last night."

"I doubt there were any right words for me last night."

"It's over."

"Forgotten?"

He grinned. "Let me show you around the house."

She released the breath she was holding. "I'd like that."

Rowe swept his arm wide. "The kitchen's back there and the dining room is next to it. I'm having an extra-long table built for the dining room, and a dozen chairs."

"A dozen?"

A grin played at the edges of his mouth. "You think we'll have more children?"

"Oh, no. That's plenty."

His gaze lingered on her a beat longer before he

led her into the front room. A large stone hearth dominated the west wall. "This is the front room. For guests. The other room can serve as a spare bedroom, parlor, whatever you like."

"I thought maybe a library."

"If that's what you want."

"Are you sure?" She couldn't keep the excitement from her voice.

"It's your house too, Jenna."

Touched, and pleased beyond reason, she hugged him tight, girlish excitement bubbling inside her, before she hurried into the unfinished room. "I've always wanted a library of my own."

Rowe folded his arms over his chest and leaned against the doorjamb. "I'll work on the shelves this winter. No doubt those crates of books I unloaded a few weeks ago and stored in the barn will fill every inch of wall space."

His kindness roused her insecurities. "Are you sure? You've given me so much already, and I've done nothing for you."

"You've done a lot."

A nervous laugh rumbled in her throat. "Like given you indigestion."

He didn't smile as he reached out and brushed a stray lock from her forehead. "You've brought me into your life, given me the chance to be a part of a family."

She shook her head. "I don't have much practice being a part of a family myself, at least not a normal one. Mine wasn't the closest."

"Maybe, but that hasn't stopped you from caring. You protect Kate with your life, and nobody has ever tried so hard to bake biscuits for me."

The man had her emotions teetering on a tightrope. One minute she was angry, the next wanting nothing but his touch. And in the next second she was humbled and speechless. It struck her that this fierce-looking rancher who towered over most men had never had anyone to worry over him. "What about your mother? Didn't she cook for you?"

"Never knew her."

The matter-of-fact words conjured sad images of a motherless child. "She died?"

"Left. My father said she was selfish, cared only about herself. Other people in town said she was too young. I'll never know the truth."

"And your father?" she whispered.

"The last memory I have of him is dropping me off at the mission school. I never saw him again."

"How old were you?"

"Ten." Rowe shrugged, as if dismissing the old pain like a worn coat.

Jenna knew how the past could haunt a person. With her own parents' abandonment still so fresh, she understood the pain, the bewilderment, the isolation. Yet she'd been a fully grown woman with some resources. He'd been just a child.

"Rowe, I'm so sorry."

He held up his hand. "Ancient history."

It wasn't, but she wouldn't argue the point. She understood what it had cost him to confide in her. The deepest emotions always proved the most difficult to put into words. She squeezed his arm and smiled. "Show me the upstairs."

His gaze nailed her and for an instant understanding connected them. "With pleasure."

He took her elbow and guided her up the stairs. There were five bedrooms on the second floor—four small ones and a large one that faced east. In the master bedroom, a rumpled pallet and blanket lay in the corner. Guilt tugged at Jenna when she thought about how she'd driven him out of their bedroom last night.

"What do you think?" His rough voice forced her back to the present.

"The house is nearly built. I can't believe you've done so much." Despite unfinished walls, she imagined rugs warming the floors, pictured small beds and toys.

He leaned against the wall in the largest room. Bright sunlight streamed in through the window next to him. "I started on the house six months ago. Managed to get the walls up by the end of the summer, figuring we'd be in by spring.''

She traced her hand along the window frame. ''The house looks as if it's ahead of schedule.''

A ghost of a smile touched his lips. ''Poured myself into it these last few weeks. Afraid if I didn't I wouldn't be able to keep my hands off you.''

A slow heat burned her cheeks as she thought about his hands touching her.

A year ago, she'd have run from such a powerful, earthy man. But he had quickly become the center of her life, almost as if she were falling in love with him. She shook off the thought. Yes, he stirred dark, primitive desires inside her, but love—that was an entirely different matter. Love brought heady highs and crushing lows, and she'd sworn during the months alone in Alexandria, when Everett had refused to see her, that she'd never give her heart again.

No, she didn't love Rowe, but she trusted him. And trust was more important than love. Perhaps that's why she was so drawn to him physically, why she always wanted to touch him.

She moved closer to him, until her skirts brushed his pants, and took his face in her hands. She felt the tension. He swallowed, his fists clenched at his sides as he stood very still, almost afraid to move.

"Thank you," she whispered.

His gaze unwavering, he leaned his cheek against her hand as if her touch brought pleasure and pain. "Jenna, I've done everything in my power to honor my promise not to make love to you for one month. But I'll never make it the next ten days if you don't leave now."

A rational woman would run.

"I don't want to leave," she whispered.

"I promised you I'd wait." The words seemed wrenched from his throat. "And I always keep my promises."

Jenna traced his lips with her thumb. She'd never wanted to be touched by a man so much. "Unpromise."

His face tightened. "Leave now, Jenna." His deep voice held a note of warning.

"No."

His eyes focused on her in a way that made her body quiver. "I can wait."

"Which makes me want you more."

Rowe needed no more encouragement. He pulled her into his arms and kissed her. With barely restrained fever, he pressed her against the wall, leaning his body and hardness into her. He trailed kisses along the soft column of her throat, inching lower with each kiss until he reached the soft mounds of her breasts.

She could barely breathe. Passion coursed through her body as she wove her fingers through his dark hair. Holding back hurt.

He slid his palm down her waist, cupping her buttock in his powerful hand. She sucked in a breath when she glimpsed the naked desire glimmering in his eyes.

"You are beautiful," he whispered.

His words touched her soul. In his arms, she did feel beautiful. There was no past, no future, only now. Silent, she trailed her hands down his chest, across his flat belly. With a boldness she hadn't known she possessed, she smoothed her hand over his hardness.

He captured her hand and drew it to his lips. "Not yet," he growled, his eyes sparking with devilish excitement. "I don't want this over before it starts."

He cupped her face in his hands, his eyes focused on her. "We should go back to the house. We've a proper bed for this."

She feared that if they waited they would lose this emotion-charged moment. "What better place than our new home?"

He pulled her down with him to the pallet. When she rolled on her back, he straddled her. She stroked the outside of his denim-clad thighs, and he looked as if he teetered on the brink of madness as he stared down at her.

He fisted his hands in her hair. "You deserve silk sheets."

"Silk is cold."

He let out a sigh and kissed her, branding her. "The future begins for us today," he said.

"And the past is forgotten," she whispered.

Rowe pushed up Jenna's skirts and unloosened the drawstring of her pantaloons. She raised her hips so he could slide them down her legs,

When Rowe touched her at her intimate juncture, she gasped. He teased her velvety folds with his thumb and she arched against him, moaning.

"God, Jenna, you are more than I ever dreamed of."

She nearly wept with wanting. Pressure built inside her and she drew close to the abyss she so desperately wanted to lose herself in. But just as she glimpsed true pleasure, Rowe pulled back. She whimpered in protest.

"Please." Her voice was husky, full of emotion. How could she make him understand what she wanted him to do?

"Soon," he breathed against her ear.

She smoothed her hand over his buttocks and along his thigh. She heard the sharp hiss of breath through his teeth, saw the muscles strain in his neck.

He took her hand and pressed it against his manhood, which was straining against denim. Burning with passion, she cupped him with her fingers.

"I want to make this last, but God, I want you," he said.

Helpless, she abandoned all ladylike decorum. "Don't make me wait." Her voice was a husky whisper.

The muscles and veins in his neck pulsed, then he released a ragged sigh, surrendering. He pulled back, unfastened the buttons on his pants and shoved them down over his lean hips.

Jenna didn't dare lower her gaze to his nakedness, fearing the sight would strip away her nerve. She trailed her hand along his flat belly and opened her legs.

He positioned himself, his jaw clenched. Then, without hesitation, he thrust into Jenna. She clutched his shoulders and sucked in a breath, overwhelmed not by the sensations of pleasure, but of pain as he ripped through the unexpected barrier.

Rowe froze. Still inside her, his body tensed. He stared into her eyes, surprise and anger chiseled on his granite features. Sweat glistened on his brow. "You are a virgin."

She desperately wanted to deny his claim and avoid the hundreds of questions to follow. Instead of speaking, she molded herself to him. "Make love to me."

Need and anger strained his sinewy muscles as he searched her face. "Who are you?"

The distrust she saw in his eyes nearly broke her heart. "Just Jenna." She moved. The pain had receded, replaced by desire.

With a groan born of layers of agony, he withdrew and rolled off her. He stood and yanked up his pants.

Jenna pushed herself up. His rumpled hair hung over blazing eyes and his jaw pulsed. She wanted him to take her in his arms again and hold her close, but his stance was so rigid, she realized that wasn't going to happen.

His gaze flickered over her creamy white thighs, now stained with blood. His frown deepened. She righted her skirts, feeling suddenly cold, ashamed. She fastened her bodice.

His expression dark, he muttered an oath. "Kate can't be your child."

Traitorous tears welled in her eyes. She hated the anger in his. "She's my niece."

He shoved his fingers through his hair. His scrutiny made her skin itch. "Victoria's child?"

She winced. "Yes."

"Why didn't you tell me?"

Jenna had nearly forgotten about the scandal these last few weeks, but now it all came crashing back. "I was afraid you wouldn't marry me if you knew. No one in Alexandria would have anything to do with us, because Kate was born out of wedlock."

He cursed.

"I'd thought we'd have t-time to get to know each other b-before the wedding," she stammered. "But everything was so rushed and I never could seem to find the right way to tell you. Later, everything that happened in Virginia seemed so far away. I thought maybe if I could just be the perfect wife, I wouldn't have to tell you."

"I'd have figured out you were a virgin sooner or later," he spat.

"I was hoping you wouldn't care, that maybe you'd even be pleased."

His face hardened. "You should have told me the truth."

"I was afraid. My parents left town in shame right after Victoria's death, and refused to have anything to do with Kate. Everett, my fiancé, wouldn't see me or answer my letters as long as I had Kate. So many people had turned their backs on me, and I couldn't risk you doing the same."

Rowe strode over to the window. He didn't stare

at the rolling landscape, but at the calluses on his palm. "You know me well enough now to know I don't give a tinker's damn about a society scandal."

"Yes. Now, I know."

With his back to her, he said, "Would you have married me if there hadn't been a scandal?"

She wanted to say she'd have married him no matter what, but that wouldn't have been the truth.

"No more lies, Jenna."

If she ever hoped to make up for her lies, she had to be honest with him now. "No."

His massive shoulders straightened and he raised his head. As he stared off at the horizon, he slammed his palm into the wall by the window and shouted a savage oath.

Chapter Twelve

Jenna was taken aback by the primitive anger etched in Rowe's face when he turned to face her. Rage darkened his eyes until they'd become black orbs devoid of every emotion.

She slowly rose to her feet and righted her skirts. "Rowe, let me explain."

"Not now." He jerked his head toward the horizon. "Smoke."

Caught off balance by the shift, Jenna followed his line of sight to the tendrils of smoke snaking up in the distance. The gray-black, cottony wisps foretold only trouble.

Rowe strapped on his gun belt. "Damn that Boone."

Jenna's hand trembled as she brushed her hair off her face. "Where's it coming from?"

"The Holts' ranch."

Panic sliced her insides. "Oh, dear God. Do you think he's hurt them?"

Rowe took her elbow and started toward the stairs. "It's his style. Let's get back to the house."

His tone was distant, and she so desperately wanted to bridge the gap between them. But now was not the time. Past lies and sins would have to wait until they knew the Holts were safe.

When they reached the front compound, Cisco, Blue and Pappy had already gathered. Their horses were saddled, along with Rowe's.

Pappy handed Kate to Jenna. "You see the smoke?" he said to Rowe.

Rowe opened the chamber of his pistol, checked the bullets, then snapped it closed. "Yeah. That son of a bitch, Boone."

The transformation in Pappy and the other men startled Jenna. Though she'd glimpsed their harder side when Boone had faced Rowe, their easygoing nature had allowed her to forget that survival in this land required ruthlessness. "How do you know Boone is behind this?" she asked.

Rowe's jaw tightened. "Matt Holt told me Boone cut across his property last week. He didn't do anything illegal, but he made certain Matt knew he was there."

"Boone knows you're friends with the Holts,"

Blue said. "He wouldn't be so foolish as to go after them."

"It's exactly why he would go after them," Rowe said.

Pappy spat, then ground the spittle into the dirt with his scuffed boot. "If we ride hard we can be there by sundown."

Rowe nodded. "My thoughts exactly. Mount up."

"I hope Boone ain't done nothing to those folks," Cisco said. "They're good people."

Rowe's gaze narrowed. "I'll hang him where he stands if he has." He turned to Blue. "I want you to stay behind and watch over Jenna."

Blue touched the brim of his hat. "Yes, sir."

"Anybody steps foot on my land that you don't recognize, shoot 'em."

"Will do, Boss."

Jenna hugged the baby close. "Shouldn't you go into town and get the sheriff?"

Rowe jerked on his gloves and put on his range coat. "We don't have time to go after the sheriff. And I don't want Boone's trail getting cold."

Jenna pictured Laura's bright moon-face and warm smile. "You're expecting trouble, aren't you?"

Rowe tightened the cinch on his saddle. "Yes."

With a shiver of dread, she moved to him and

pressed her fingertips to his chest, where she felt the rapid beat of his heart. "Be careful. He could be there, waiting for you."

Rowe glanced down at her fingers, then stepped back, breaking the connection. He put on his hat, tugged it low over his eyes. "I can take care of myself."

Her lies had obviously hurt Rowe deeply, and Jenna prayed that when he came back she could make it up to him. "I'll wait up."

He mounted his horse. "Don't bother. I don't know how long I'll be. Blue will keep a watch out, and if you need anything, go to him."

A cold chill danced down her spine. "Of course."

Rowe twisted the reins around his gloved hand. "Stay inside with the door bolted."

"I will." The cold wind whisked around her, pricking her face and cutting through the meager protection of her wool shawl.

Rowe's low-crowned hat shadowed his eyes and his range coat billowed in the wind. His gaze lingered on her, but it was cold and withdrawn. She hated seeing him like this—hated more that she was responsible.

She straightened her shoulders, summoning all her dignity. "We'll be waiting."

A flicker of emotion passed over his face. He

removed his hat and smoothed back his hair, then resettled the hat on his head.

"No need to worry. Kate and I know how to take care of ourselves," Jenna added.

He frowned as if the notion bothered him, then touched the tip of his Stetson with a hand that trembled—so slightly she wondered if she'd imagined it.

They rode hard, but they were too late.

By the time they'd arrived at the Holts' cabin, it was little more than ashes. Smoke drifted up from the charred beams and hot embers, which still hissed and popped in the cool afternoon air.

"Where are Laura and Matt?" Pappy asked. His weathered face had aged ten years in minutes.

"I don't know." Rowe stood in the spot that had once been the Holts' front porch. He searched the cinders, looking for signs of their bodies. When he found none, he closed his eyes and said a word of thanks.

Three weeks ago, he'd sat on this porch with Matt, savoring a cigar. They'd just enjoyed one of Laura's delicious suppers and talked about cattle prices. That night Matt had surprised Laura with three new robin's-egg-blue ribbons from the mercantile, the gift a special treat to celebrate their tenth wedding anniversary. Laura had kissed Matt fully on the lips, her eyes alight with the promise of more when they went to bed later.

Now the Holts were missing.

Sudden, sharp images of Jenna trapped in a burning cabin slashed across Rowe's mind. Fury, keen and raw, knotted his chest before he shoved aside the unbearable picture.

"You think it was just bad luck—an accident maybe?" Cisco asked.

Rowe spotted shell casings peppering the ground, shimmering in the fading light. He squatted and picked them up, rattled them in his palm. The desire for revenge singed his veins. "This was no accident."

"Think Boone's behind it?" Cisco said.

"Yes." Rowe shoved the shells in his pocket. He stared at the flame-ravaged timbers, vowing never to forget or stop searching for the man responsible.

"Maybe Laura and Matt're hiding out," Cisco offered.

Rowe stood. "There's a stand of grass over that way near a dry gulch. Let's have a look."

The three men strode toward the grassy ridge a hundred paces from the house. In truth, Rowe didn't expect much. It wasn't like Boone to leave people behind—alive.

They'd walked ten paces when Rowe spotted

flecks of blood dotting the hard ground. He knelt down and pinched the sticky fluid between his fingertips. "It's fresh."

"Think it's Laura's or Matt's?" Cisco asked.

"I hope not," Rowe said.

"Maybe they got clean away," Cisco murmured.

"Matt would know I'd see the smoke. He wouldn't have gone far," Rowe said.

He scanned the endless grasslands, the jutting mountains in the distance. "Let's spread out. We only have a few hours of daylight left, and if they're alive we're gonna have to hurry."

The three men fanned out and started their search. Five minutes later, Cisco found Matt in the ravine, curled on his side, his eyes closed. "Boss, I found Matt. I think he's dead!"

Rowe hurried down the dirt bank. His head pounded as he knelt beside Matt and gently rolled him onto his back. Dirt and sweat caked his friend's too-still face and a large bloodstain tinged his gut and right thigh. For a moment, Rowe had to remind himself to breathe.

"Everyone in the valley liked Matt," Cisco said. "Hell, he didn't even like to carry a gun."

"Whoever shot him done it in cold blood," Pappy muttered, taking off his hat.

"Damn it to hell," Rowe said, bowing his head.

Cisco yanked off his hat, too. "He was a good man."

Pappy knelt beside the lanky man's body. He placed his forefingers on Matt's neck. "He still is."

Rowe's head snapped up. "He's alive?"

Grim-faced, Pappy started to unbutton Matt's shirt. He winced when he looked at the bullet hole. "Barely. We've got to get him to town, if he's going to have any kind of chance."

Rowe refused to offer his thanks yet. "We've got to find Laura. Cisco, hitch your horse to the Holts' wagon. Pappy, do what you can for Matt. I'll search for her."

His heart drummed in his chest as he started running down the ditch, and he thought he'd go mad with frustration. Then he saw the flutter of calico near a clump of bushes. He reached Laura in seconds and dropped to his knees beside her. Gingerly, he turned her over. Blood caked her left temple, but she was breathing.

Rowe wasted no time on prayer, but scooped her up in his arms and carried her back toward the remains of the house. There, Cisco and Pappy had already laid Matt in the wagon bed and were hitching up Cisco's horse.

"She's alive," Rowe called out.

Cisco hurried to Rowe and helped him carry

Laura to the wagon where they laid her limp body beside her husband. For such strong, vibrant people, they looked so pale and fragile.

Rowe understood that life could turn sour in the blink of an eye, but it never failed to sicken him when tragedy struck a friend.

Pappy pulled a blanket from his saddlebag and laid it over them. "We best hurry."

Rowe closed the wagon's tailgate. His soul ached as he stared helplessly at his friends. "Pappy, tend to their wounds. Cisco, you drive."

The best thing Rowe could do for his friends now was to track Boone into hell.

"You two go to my ranch. Pick up Jenna, Kate and whatever supplies you need. I'll meet you in town soon as I can."

Pappy squeezed Rowe's shoulder. "Where are you going?"

"After Boone."

"That's a bad idea, Rowe."

Rowe curled his fingers into fists. "Now's not the time to argue with me."

"Like hell it isn't. I'm not letting you go off half-cocked."

Rowe itched to drive his fists into Boone's gut. Until he did, anyone who got in his way wasn't safe. "I give the orders around here."

"It's nearly dark," Pappy reasoned. "It'll be impossible to track Boone and his men at night."

"Finding men like him is what I do best."

"You'll be riding into an armed compound. Those cutthroats will kill anything that comes close."

"I'll get in."

"Yeah, you just might, but you got a snowball's chance in hell of getting out in one piece."

"I want Boone."

Pappy swore. "I ain't following you to your grave. And that's exactly where you'll be if you let your fury blind you. We need to take care of Matt and Laura first. Revenge will come later."

Reflex made Rowe raise his fist. "That monster gunned down my friends like they were animals."

Unflinching, Pappy glared up at Rowe. "And we'll get him tomorrow, when we've got daylight and cool heads."

"I'm going—*now*." Rowe wrapped the reins of his horse around his hand. "Cisco, get moving." He glared at the young man, daring him to argue.

Cisco's questioning gaze darted to Pappy, but loyalty overruled reason. "Sure, Boss."

"Boone's waiting for you and you know it," Pappy said. "If you're going to catch him, you'll need ice water in your veins, not fire."

"Let it go, Pappy."

"Let's say by some miracle you get past Boone's men and kill him, then what? You'll be tried and convicted of cold-blooded murder."

Rowe didn't need proof to hunt Boone down, kill him where he stood, but the law did. He lusted for frontier justice, not courts, lawyers and jails. "Sheriff Donelly will never arrest me. He knows Boone is scum."

"He's a lawman, bound by the law, not friendship." Pappy grabbed hold of Rowe's reins. "Who's gonna take care of Kate and Jenna if you get yourself killed?"

Jenna. The mention of her name stirred emotions Rowe didn't dare dwell on. He thought back to the shock that had overtaken him when he'd discovered her virginity. She'd lied to him. He'd worked so hard to gain her trust these last few weeks, and she'd lied to him. "I'm not going to get myself killed."

"Don't take any foolish chances. For the first time in your life you've got exactly what you've always wanted—a fine woman, a child and the promise of a bright future. Don't throw it away."

Pappy's words struck a raw nerve. This morning when he'd woken up, he'd have agreed with the old man. Now he couldn't say for certain what he had or didn't have.

* * *

What if Rowe didn't come home...

A biting cold shuddered through Jenna each time she thought of Rowe leaving her. She'd accepted her parents' desertion, and Everett's, but the idea that Rowe might leave her was too much to bear.

Jenna stared out the cabin window into the night. A single lantern hung by the back door, its feeble light little protection against the endless darkness.

Restless, she walked to the hearth, and stretched out her hands to the blazing fire. The flames danced high, warming her palms and face. She breathed in deeply, willing the constricted muscles in her chest to relax.

"He's coming home," she whispered.

And when he did, she would tell him the whole truth about Kate, her own past. Jenna only prayed that he'd forgive her lies and not send her away.

She hugged her arms around her chest. When she'd accepted Rowe's marriage proposal, she'd assumed that she would be in firm control of her emotions. Theirs was supposed to be a business agreement of sorts. Companionship and mutual respect were all she'd bargained for.

Yet from the moment she'd first seen him on that dusty street, she'd been off-kilter. He stirred feelings so deep and primal, there were moments she didn't recognize herself. She'd acted out of control, wanton even, just as Victoria had. Jenna had given in to emotions, when good sense dictated otherwise.

She'd spent her life surrounded by people, yet until she'd met Rowe, she hadn't realized how empty and lonely her life was. And now this precious treasure was slipping through her fingers like sand. She wanted nothing more than for him to take her in his arms and finish what they'd started today.

She'd tried so hard to be the perfect wife, worrying over laundry and cooking, when in fact she'd overlooked the most important quality of a wife. Honesty.

Raising her chin, Jenna decided that somehow she'd find a way to fix this mess she'd created. Rowe might not ever learn to love her, but he would trust her.

It would take time to rebuild the trust he'd given her readily at first. But she had time. She wasn't going anywhere.

The rumble of wagon wheels and the deep timbre of men's voices startled Jenna from her thoughts. She hurried to the window and shoved back the curtain.

Rowe, his face shadowed by his hat, climbed off

his horse and tied his reins to the wagon. His shoulders slumped slightly.

Relief flooded her body. She threw back the bar on the door and yanked it open. "Rowe!"

He lifted his head at the sound of his name. Thick stubble on his square jaw, emphasized the dark shadows under his eyes.

She hurried down the front steps, meeting him halfway. "Thank God you're all right," she whispered as she embraced him. "How are the Holts?"

Rowe didn't hug her back.

Jenna dropped her arms and stepped away from the welcome warmth of his body. "Rowe?"

"Get Kate. You're both leaving."

Chapter Thirteen

Rowe wanted to send her away.

Jenna could feel the blood drain from her face just as it had done when her parents and then Everett had turned against her.

"Why? I don't understand." Her breath hitched in her throat and she struggled to shore up her defenses.

"The Holts. They've been shot. I've got them in the wagon."

Shock rose like bile. "Are they alive?"

"Barely."

Jenna froze when she looked past him into the wagon bed and got her first look at the Holts. Their skin was so pale, their bodies so still. She feared she was already too late even as she climbed aboard the wagon and inspected Matt's bandaged gut. "Has there been a lot of bleeding?"

"No," Pappy said.

"Let's hope it's not internal."

"You know more about medicine than stitching cuts," Rowe said. Jenna didn't miss the edge in his voice.

"I worked in the mission hospital in Virginia several times a week for almost two years. I've seen my share of illness and gunshot wounds. I didn't bring much with me from Virginia, but I do have some medicines, and after your fall I made a point of rolling bandages. I'll get them."

She didn't wait for his response, but climbed down and hurried inside. Moments later she returned with a satchel full of supplies. She found Pappy, Blue and Rowe by the open tailgate, staring grimly at their friends.

Jenna set her basket of supplies down on the wagon bed and started to climb aboard. Immediately, Rowe took her arm and helped her up.

"Pappy," she said breathlessly as she knelt beside Laura. "Bundle Kate up. Pack cans of milk, her bottles and diapers. When she's ready we'll leave."

"Yes, ma'am."

Jenna smoothed back Laura's hair from the bullet wound. Dampening a cloth with rubbing alcohol, she cleaned the gash. To her relief, she discovered the bullet had only grazed Laura's skull, not penetrated it.

She opened a bottle of smelling salts and waved it under Laura's nose. The woman's head twitched back and forth and she moaned softly, fighting the foul odor and consciousness.

Rowe leaned over the side of the wagon. "She's coming around."

Jenna ran her fingers through Laura's hair until she found the bump she'd suspected was there. "The bullet only grazed her. Likely the force of it knocked her down, and she hit her head when she fell. Whoever did this to her must have assumed she was dead."

"Thank God," Rowe whispered.

Laura moaned and then her eyes fluttered open. "Matt."

Jenna smiled. "He's here. He's alive. I'll take care of him. You just rest."

"They shot him," Laura whimpered.

"I know. But we'll look after him."

Tears trailed down Laura's face. Her hands slid to her belly. "My baby."

Jenna squeezed Laura's hand and glanced down at her friend's skirts. "There's no sign of bleeding. Just rest."

Laura's eyes drifted closed and she slipped back into unconsciousness.

As Jenna turned her attention to Matt, Rowe touched her shoulder. She glanced up at him and for a moment the connection between them flickered to life. "What does she mean by 'my baby'?" he asked.

"Laura's pregnant."

The lines around his mouth deepened. "Matt never said anything."

"He doesn't know. Laura wanted to be farther along before she told him."

Rowe rubbed the back of his neck. "They've wanted a baby for so long."

"They still have a good chance of seeing their child born." She prodded Matt's wound with her fingertip, felt the bullet embedded there. It was less than an inch deep, but she didn't have the skill to remove it.

"Are you a trained nurse?"

It was a relief not to hide her past any longer, not to have to think before she spoke. "No, but I learned a great deal from my former fiancé, who is a doctor. He donated his time and I accompanied him often."

"Fiancé." Rowe snorted. "Everett?"

She reached for fresh bandages. "Yes."

He shoved away from the wagon, nearly bumping into Pappy, who'd arrived with Kate and a bagful of supplies.

"We're ready to go," the old man said.

Rowe glanced at the sleeping child, then tucked the blanket tighter around her face. "Good."

"After we get to town, what are you going to do?" Pappy asked him.

"I'm going to find Boone and kill him."

Rowe rode beside the wagon, where Jenna watched over the Holts throughout the journey. Pappy tended a sleeping Kate, while Blue drove the buckboard. Cisco had ridden ahead to alert the doctor that they were coming.

They traveled as fast as they could, but each bump and rut in the road made Matt groan with pain.

Jenna's medical skills and cool confidence surprised Rowe. He'd half expected her to run at the sight of trouble, but she hadn't. Each time he looked at her, it was as if he saw a stranger.

Miserably, he remembered the first letter he'd received from her. Everything about the letter had surprised him, from its fine cream paper to the delicate script. He'd thought perhaps that she'd made a mistake writing him; what would a lady want with a weathered cowhand like himself?

But he'd responded to her that very day, anxious to know more. He'd half expected never to hear from her again, but that hadn't stopped him from checking the mail two or three times a week. Nor had it silenced the loud whoop he'd given when her second letter arrived. When he'd received her telegram accepting his marriage offer, he'd reread the paper a half-dozen times before he let himself believe it.

Hell, if he hadn't been so afraid of losing her, he'd not have rushed the wedding ceremony.

She'd just seemed too good to be true, and he hadn't wanted to let her slip through his fingers.

He tightened his hold on the reins now, and forced his thoughts back to the present. First Boone, then Jenna.

He'd have to work quickly if he were going to catch Boone before the snows made the trails impassable. He was anxious to begin the hunt, eager to taste revenge.

The sun hung low in the sky by the time the wagon reached town. The muddy main street bustled with people and wagons, but everyone cleared a path for Rowe's party. Down the street a half-dozen men had gathered with saddled horses. They'd donned range coats, hats and pistols, evidence that Cisco had arrived and alerted them. The riders' saddlebags bulged with supplies, obviously stocked for a long journey.

Many townsfolk stopped what they were doing and tried to peer into the wagon as it passed. Rowe knew they were full of questions and worries, but he didn't stop to talk.

Doc Carter waited on the boardwalk in front of his clinic. The doctor was old and looked frail, but his voice was clear and strong when he spoke. "Get 'em inside so I can have a look."

Jenna, with Kate in her arms, trailed behind as Rowe, Pappy and Cisco carried Matt into the small examining room. Matt's face was as white as the cotton sheet on the bed, but thanks to Jenna, he was alive.

An antiseptic smell filled the simply furnished, but clean clinic. It was outfitted with an examining table, three cots and a large cabinet with glass doors. Inside the cabinet, brown medicine bottles lined the top two shelves. On the bottom three shelves, clean surgical instruments lay on pristine cotton sheets.

Laura moaned softly as Rowe carried her into the clinic and laid her on a cot near Matt.

Doc Carter rolled up his sleeves as he moved toward Matt. "Who bandaged him?"

Jenna shifted a sleeping Kate to her other shoulder. "I did."

Doc Carter's gray mustache twitched as he studied her. "You might have saved his life."

"I pray they make it," she whispered.

"You folks best get comfortable. It's gonna be a long day," the doctor said.

Rowe knew there was nothing else for him to do here. Matt and Laura were in good hands, and Jenna and Kate were safe. His time was now best spent tracking Boone.

Rowe backed toward the door. "I'll leave you to your work."

Jenna grabbed his sleeve as he stepped out onto the boardwalk. "Rowe!"

He stopped, but didn't turn to face her. "I've got to leave."

"I know this is not the time, but we need to talk."

"There's nothing to say." His voice was hoarse, strained.

"There's a lot to say."

One of the men near the jail rechecked his rifle, then shoved it into his saddle holster. His horse pawed the ground, anxious to get moving and ease the chill from its muscles. Several men mounted up and called out to Rowe.

Rowe cursed. "I'll be right there," he called. His expression darkened. "Check yourself into the hotel. We'll talk when I get back, Jenna."

"Rowe, please, don't leave like this."

He expelled a breath. "Jenna, the last thing I want to do right now is talk. Yes, I'm angry that you lied, and yes, I've got a lot of thinking to do about *us*. But I've got a snowstorm headed this way and a madman to catch. Time to talk is a luxury I just don't have.''

Even with all that had passed between them, he hated the hurt in her eyes. But there was nothing to be done about it now. Turning, he strode toward his horse, untied the reins and mounted.

Several members of the posse glanced at Rowe, took in his murderous expression. No one pressed him for conversation.

Jenna watched Rowe and the other men ride down the main street toward the hills until they disappeared from sight. She'd always figured telling Rowe the truth would be awkward, but she'd never guessed it would be devastating.

Her shoulders slumped as she tipped her head back, trying to stem the tide of tears that threatened. ''You've mucked things up real well, Jenna,'' she whispered. ''How are you ever gonna fix it when—*if*—he returns?''

''He'll be back,'' Mrs. Brown said from behind her. The older woman wore a dark brown coat that hugged her round frame. Tiny curls peaked out from her cap, framing her rosy, round face.

Embarrassed that she'd made a scene in public,

Jenna could manage only a weak smile. "I didn't realize you were there."

"Didn't mean to eavesdrop, but I couldn't help but overhear. Don't you worry, dear, I've felt the brunt of Rowe Mercer's temper from time to time and have survived to tell the tale. Man's bark is worse than his bite."

"I hope you're right."

"Of course I'm right. Now let's get you and that baby back to my house, where you can warm up. It's too cold to stand around outside."

"I shouldn't leave Laura and Matt."

"If anyone can save them, it's Doc Carter. Mean as a snake but the best doctor I've met. Now let's get home."

"Rowe said to check into the hotel."

"Hotel! I won't hear of it."

Wordlessly, Jenna nodded her thanks, grateful not to be alone. She followed Mrs. Brown down the boardwalk to her clapboard house at the edge of the town. Orange light from the setting sun glowed on a simple white fence, which encircled her yard, and the house looked as if it had been freshly whitewashed. Inside, the decor was completely feminine. The house was packed with furniture—settees decorated with doilies and tables covered with dainty figurines. A cuckoo clock ticked nosily from its perch on the wall above a porcelain-topped table near a potbellied stove. The place smelled cozy, like cinnamon and vanilla. And Jenna felt herself relax despite her worries.

Kate started to stir, rubbing her fists on her eyes. She raised her head, looked at Jenna and presented her with a lopsided, gooey smile.

"Let me hold her while you get your cloak off," Mrs. Brown said.

Jenna handed Kate to Mrs. Brown and quickly pulled off her coat, hung it on a rack by the door, then tugged off her gloves and tucked them in her coat pocket.

Mrs. Brown rubbed her nose to Kate's. "Why, you're just as pretty as a picture."

On cue, Kate frowned and started to fuss.

Jenna took the baby and jostled her. "I'm afraid she's hungry."

"Of course she is. Let me show you to your room so you can nurse her."

Jenna hesitated. There seemed no escaping her lie. "I use a bottle."

"Poor dear, milk never came in?"

Feeling the familiar twinge of guilt, she could only shrug.

Mrs. Brown scooted Jenna toward the kitchen. "Well, come on in and have yourself a seat. I've a few cans of milk, and if you give me your bottle, I'll have you fixed up in no time."

Jenna retrieved Kate's bottle, which she kept wrapped in cheesecloth in her purse. She was happy to hand it to Mrs. Brown and let her fill it. Jenna's mind was still so cluttered with the last few moments she'd spent with Rowe. His anger haunted her, and she knew there'd be no peace until she'd dealt with it.

"Mrs. Brown, you're very kind."

"We look out for each other here in Saddler Creek. Each of us was a newcomer at one point." Mrs. Brown opened a can of milk, poured it into a pan on the stove then went to the sink and pumped fresh water over the bottle, rinsing it completely.

Jenna took a seat at the large kitchen table. She shifted Kate to her lap and began to bounce her gently. "Have you lived in Saddler Creek most of your life?"

Mrs. Brown set a plate of scones on the table and an earthenware crock filled with strawberry jam. "Good heavens, no. The town's not even twenty years old. No, Mr. Brown and I came out here in '61. We'd lost our oldest in the war and both of us needed a change. I think I told you that Mr. Brown owns the mercantile."

"Yes."

She retreated to the stove to stir the milk heating in the saucepan. Silence hung between them as she poured the milk-molasses mixture into the bottle and fastened the nipple.

Mrs. Brown handed over the bottle, then draped a tea cloth over Jenna's shoulder. As she stared down at Kate, the sparkle in her eyes returned. "Mind telling me how you and Rowe met? We've all wondered how you two could ever have crossed paths."

Jenna tucked Kate in the crook of her arm, tested the milk on the tender side of her wrist and, finding it the right temperature, put the bottle in the baby's mouth. The child cupped the bottle in her hands, greedily sucking in the milk. "I responded to an ad he placed in the *Alexandria Gazette*."

Mrs. Brown's thick eyebrows shot up. "We get our fair share of mail-order brides out here. The men are lonely and marriageable women are scarce. But why would a lovely girl like you respond? I can't believe the men back East weren't lined up to meet you."

"I wanted a fresh start."

The older woman studied her before she picked up a fat scone and broke it open. "This town may not offer as many luxuries as back home, but fresh starts are plentiful."

"Sometimes I wonder if you can ever really be rid of the past."

"The past is like a bad dream. You may not ever forget it, but in time its power fades."

"You make it sound easy."

"Nothing worth having is easy. But until the past does fade, nothing distracts better than a warm scone," she said cheerily. She smeared a generous spoonful of jam on it and set it in front of Jenna.

"They smell wonderful. I've not had a scone in months."

Mrs. Brown sprinkled tea leaves into a Wedgwood teapot, poured hot water over them, and sat down at the table, after setting out two matching, rose-trimmed cups. "I expect you to eat at least two. You are too thin, dear, as slender as a reed." She smiled an impish grin. "Which is why I intend to fatten you up while you're here."

The knot in Jenna's back eased. Mrs. Brown's softness made her believe she could talk to her about anything, a feeling she'd never shared with her mother.

Kate sucked greedily on the nipple and soon only bubbles remained in her bottle. Jenna set the bottle on the table, placed Kate on her shoulder and patted her back until she burped.

Mrs. Brown leaned a little closer. "I remember when Rowe moved to Saddler Creek. I don't think he spoke to a soul for the first six months. He was so determined to make a success of the Crossfire.

The man was tough as nails, knew something about farming, but didn't know the first thing about ranching. If not for Pappy, I doubt the Crossfire Ranch would have made it. Many of us thought he'd give up, but he hung in there.''

The news surprised Jenna. "He seems to know everything about everything.''

"Men are like that, dear. Generally, they're convinced they're right even when they don't have the faintest clue what they're doing.''

"I know so little about him.''

"He's never been the type to share his thoughts. Always has kept his cards close to his vest.'' She shrugged. "I suppose he's not so proud of his bounty-hunting past and wants to leave it behind.''

Jenna straightened. "Rowe was a bounty hunter?''

"Oh my, yes. He doesn't talk about it anymore, but he made his money tracking killers and bank robbers. They say he was quite ruthless. I heard tell he captured over two hundred men.''

Irritated, Jenna raised an eyebrow. To think she'd worried and worried over her own past, when all along, Rowe had his own secrets. "Funny, he never told me.''

Chapter Fourteen

The morning sun touched the lip of the horizon, casting watery light on Rowe, Sheriff Donelly, Pappy and the six other men in the posse. Flecks of snow drifted from the sky as, rifles ready, they lay on the icy hillside, staring down at the ramshackle cabin in the ravine below.

Adrift in the fading darkness, a single lantern burned there. Rowe had removed the rawhide hobbling the renegades' horses, and left the strands pooled in the snow by the cabin.

"Damn, Rowe, you must be part wolf to have sniffed out this bunch. How the hell did you find them?" Donelly asked.

"Could smell 'em a mile off," Rowe said.

Rowe had a knack for tracking. That skill, coupled with his single-minded goal to make money and buy his own spread, had made him a successful bounty hunter. But prosperity had cost him a piece of his humanity. When he'd retired eight years ago, he'd been little better than the animals he'd tracked, and he'd vowed to turn his back on the business forever. Yet it seemed that each time he thought he'd escaped the past, someone like Boone dragged him back.

"I reckon there's a thousand dollars worth of reward money sitting in that cabin," Donelly said.

"It's yours," Rowe said.

"You found 'em."

"I'm here for Boone, not the money."

Donelly pushed back his hat. "The posse and I will split the reward money then, if you don't mind."

They could burn it for all he cared. "Fine."

"I'm surprised they didn't come a-running when the horses ran away," the sheriff whispered. He brushed back a thick lock of hair from his smooth-skinned face.

Rowe looked at Donelly and wondered if he'd ever been that young. "Likely they got drunk last night and are still sleeping it off."

"Kinda sloppy, don't you think?"

"Why should they be worried?" Rowe said. "As far as they know, they've gotten away with murder and have all the time in the world."

"I can't wait to see the expressions on their

faces when they realize their horses are gone.'' The sheriff's zeal underscored his youth.

''Don't rush until I say so,'' Rowe warned. By rights the sheriff had jurisdiction, but sometime during the night, the younger man had deferred to Rowe's age and experience. ''I'm not interested in seeing you or anyone else get killed.''

''No arguments here. As much as I want to break down that door and put a bullet in Boone, I won't. Like you, I got a good woman waiting for me in Saddler Creek who I aim to see again.''

Rowe squeezed his fingers around the barrel of his rifle. He'd expelled Jenna from his thoughts so his head would be clear. But allusion to her brought their last meeting roaring to life.

''Miz Jenna looked a mite sad when we rode out,'' the sheriff commented.

''Yep,'' Rowe said.

''Guess she was worried about you.''

Rowe was spared a response when the door to the cabin opened. A grizzled rustler stumbled out the door and squinted against the rising sun. He faced the cabin wall and answered nature's call before he turned again and noticed that the horses were gone.

Immediately the rustler ran into the cabin. The men's shouts could be heard all the way up the embankment.

Seconds later the other five rustlers rushed out of the cabin. Two were still strapping on their gun belts, while another tugged on his boot.

Rowe leveled his rifle as the outlaws scurried. He didn't recognize Boone in the crowd. "Damn, he's not there."

"Maybe he's inside," the sheriff whispered.

Rowe's grip tightened on the rifle barrel. "Don't count on it." He fired the first warning shot and shouted, "Drop your guns."

The rustlers drew their guns, squinting against the sun as they stared toward the jagged rocks where Rowe and the others hid. When one rustler ran back toward the cabin, Rowe fired, sending up a spray of snow in front of the man and halting his advance.

"I'll say it one more time," Rowe shouted. "Drop your weapons or I'll shoot you like ducks in a barrel."

One man spat, another kicked the ground with his foot, but none released their weapons.

Rowe's next shot knocked one rustler's hat off his head, and his third hit the silver handle of a rustler's gun as he drew it.

The outlaws dropped their weapons and put their hands in the air.

"We got 'em," the sheriff said.

Rowe cocked his rifle. "Move in slow, men, and

watch their hands. They'll do what it takes to escape.''

The posse descended from the rocky hillside, moving carefully. As the sheriff and his men gathered up the band of desperadoes, Rowe edged toward the cabin. He kicked in the front door with one swift movement and entered the darkened single room. As he'd suspected, Boone was gone.

''Is he in there?'' Pappy called out.

Rowe took one last look at the squalid cabin, then turned back toward the light. ''No.'' He strode toward the rustlers, his index finger pressing the trigger. ''Where is he?''

The six men's silence only fueled Rowe's anger and frustration. He grabbed the man closest to him by the frayed lapels of his range coat. The man smelled of dung and months of sweat.

Rowe pressed the barrel of his gun to his temple. ''Where's Boone?''

The rustler swallowed. ''Don't know. And if I did I wouldn't tell.''

Rowe chuckled, but the sound was more demonic than humorous. ''You willing to die for him?''

The rustler shifted. ''Boone's been good to us.''

''Is that a yes?'' Rowe said. He scraped the gun down the man's cheek, then cocked it.

The man glanced toward his companions.

They'd all grown pale. Then his gaze shifted to the sheriff and the posse. "You gonna let him do this? It ain't legal to shoot an unarmed man!"

Each knew and liked the Holts. None challenged Rowe or his methods.

Pappy scratched his head. "Maybe shooting's too good for 'em, Rowe. I got my knife. It guts a fish just fine. Should work on these animals just as well." To drive his point home, Pappy pulled the long knife from his boot and touched the tip with his thumb. Blood dripped to the ground.

The rustler's knees visibly weakened. "We don't know where he is. He took off yesterday."

"Where'd he go?" Rowe asked.

"Don't know."

Rowe shrugged and looked at Pappy. "Gut 'em."

As Pappy moved forward, the rustler shouted, "Leadville! He said he was going to Leadville."

Rowe hesitated, as if measuring the truth of the man's words, then he nodded. "If he ain't, I'm coming after you." He pushed the man toward the sheriff.

Within minutes, the sheriff had the outlaws on their horses, their hands tied behind their backs. He mounted his own horse and raised his hand to Rowe. "Ready?"

"I'll be along soon enough."

The sheriff nodded and, with the posse surrounding the outlaws, headed back to town. Only Pappy remained behind.

Rowe walked into the cabin, toward the small potbellied stove in the corner. With one savage kick, he knocked the stove over. Hot coals spread out on the floor, igniting the soiled blankets and the cabin's brittle wood.

Rowe strode out of the cabin and turned to watch the small shack burn. The wood cracked and popped as the fire devoured it.

Pappy dug a hand-rolled cigarette out of his pocket. He struck a match against his boot and lit the tip. "What's eating you?"

"I want Boone."

"It's more than that."

"It's nothing."

Pappy squinted as his cigarette smoke trailed up into the air. "Translation—Jenna."

"I'm not interested in talking, old-timer." The old buzzard had a way of zeroing in on raw nerves.

"Out with it, Rowe."

A sour taste settled in his mouth. The truth would come out sooner or later, whatever the hell the truth was. "She lied about her past."

Pappy remained quiet, staring at him like a buzzard.

"She's never been married. Kate belonged to

her late sister. Jenna left Virginia because of some scandal.''

Pappy stoked the patchy white stubble on his chin. ''But she is legally married to you?''

''Yes.''

''Then what's the problem?''

''Damn it, she *lied to me*,'' he shouted.

''You ain't exactly been open and honest.''

''That's different.''

''Is it?''

''She as much as admitted that she'd never have married me if her hand hadn't been forced in Virginia.''

Pappy shrugged. ''The what-ifs or might-have-beens don't matter. What matters is that she's *your wife*.'' He drew on his cigarette. ''The question is what are you going to do about it?''

Two weeks had passed since Rowe had left town. The sheriff, Pappy and the other townsmen had returned ten days earlier with the six outlaws, but Rowe hadn't been with them. Pappy had explained to Jenna that Rowe had gone after Boone, but she suspected his absence had more to do with her.

She had spent most of the last two weeks at the clinic with Laura and Matt, in the tiny back room used for patients who needed more time to mend.

Laura had recovered quickly from her wound, but the main concern had been the baby. Doc Carter had ordered strict bed rest for her, and no stress.

But worry was all Laura did while Matt's life hung in the balance for over a week. There'd been a point when the doctor had feared he'd have to amputate the rancher's leg. But Matt's health had taken a positive turn right after Laura had clutched his hand and confided that she was expecting a baby in the spring. He didn't wake up that very minute, but his fever broke within the hour and by daybreak his eyes opened and he was asking for water.

In time both would recover fully. Jenna smiled at the thought as she glanced down at Kate, who slept in a cradle lent to her by one of the women in town.

Jenna and Laura waited while Doc Carter examined Matt in the other room.

Laura tugged on a loose string dangling from the cuff of her nightgown. She stared at the closed door that led to the examining room. ''Doc's been in with Matt a long time.''

Jenna concentrated on her sewing—a new dress she was making for Laura. ''Matt's been very ill. It's a miracle he survived his wounds. The doctor's just making sure his mending continues.''

Laura managed a tentative smile. The color had

returned to her cheeks and in time the scar on her forehead would fade. "He was so sick, so fragile. I can't believe he survived."

"But he did."

Laura eased back against the pillows, but the tension remained. "I shouldn't fret. But when I think that I could have lost him it frightens me to no end."

Jenna secured her sewing needle in the fabric and set it aside. "You didn't lose him."

"Thanks to you."

"I didn't do anything."

"Doc said if you hadn't tied off the wound the way you had Matt would have bled to death."

"It's over now. You and Matt are going to be fine and that baby inside you is growing every day. Concentrate on eating and getting stronger."

Laura glanced down at her lap, where a tray held a bowl of untouched broth and bread. "You're right. But between this case of nerves and the nausea, it's all I can do to even look at food."

Jenna lifted an eyebrow. "The broth will settle your stomach. The more you don't eat, the sicker you'll feel."

Laura lifted the spoon and swirled it in the broth.

"Would it help your appetite to know that I didn't make the soup or the biscuits?"

Laura laughed. "Your cooking is not that bad."

Jenna raised an eyebrow.

Laura chuckled. "Okay, you got a thing or two to learn."

"Eat."

She sampled one small spoonful. Liking it, she took another, and then another. "It's good."

"Cora Avery from the hotel brought it by."

"She's very sweet."

"She and a half-dozen other ladies in town have been worried sick about you. All have taken turns sitting with you and Matt at night so that I could get some rest or tend to Kate. It's amazing how the folks have all banded together."

"Neighbors help neighbors."

Jenna glanced down at Kate, asleep in the cradle. "I had an interesting chat with Mrs. Brown the other day about Rowe."

Laura's eyes narrowed. "Those two don't always see eye to eye."

"Mrs. Brown didn't have anything bad to say about him."

"Really?"

"She did tell me about Rowe's bounty hunting days."

Laura's eyebrows raised. "She did?"

"Is it some kind of secret?"

"No, no. It's just that folks don't talk about it much. Rowe hates to discuss those days and, well, he's not the kind of man you prod for information.''

"What do you know about his past?"

Laura absently stirred her soup. "Matt, Rowe and I grew up together in Missouri."

"He never told me."

"Typical Rowe." She tore off a piece of bread. "My father owned a large farm, and Matt's daddy owned a smaller one nearby. Rowe lived in the town mission school. When he was twelve or thirteen, the mission folks decided Rowe was big enough to fend for himself. My daddy offered Rowe a job, which he took. Rowe worked harder than two grown men, and he learned all he could about farming. But there was a restlessness in him. He was always talking about making money, of having a spread of his own. Finally, he just took off, left a note to Daddy. I didn't think I'd ever see him again.

"I found out much later that he moved West. He developed quite a reputation as a bounty hunter. Moved around a lot in Texas and up into Colorado. Matt and I ran into him in Denver about nine years ago. We didn't recognize him, but he knew who we were. Honestly, he gave me such a start when I saw him dressed in rawhide, his hair long and wild, those pistols hanging from his hips. His eyes had grown hard, piecing almost. We told him about our spread and told him to look us up, thinking he'd never do any such thing. But the following spring he did. In fact, he bought the Crossfire land and started his own operation.''

''I don't understand why he cares about his past. He's done nothing to be ashamed of, has he?''

''No, nothing like that. I think the past is very painful for him. He said once bounty hunting nearly drained his soul dry—that he was becoming like the men he hunted.'' Laura met Jenna's gaze. ''A desperado came into town a few years back, gunning for Rowe, looking for revenge. The man called Rowe out, threatened to shoot up the town if he didn't show. Rowe showed. The two faced off. Rowe shot the outlaw clean through the heart. It was a fair fight, but I think a lot of folks realized then just how savage the dark side of Rowe was. The marriageable women were careful from then on to keep their distance.''

''He was afraid I wouldn't want him.''

''Yes.''

''He scared me at first. But there's a goodness in him. He's so good to Kate and so gentle with me. Every morning when I wake up and I see him and the mountains, I'm so glad I came to Saddler Creek and Rowe. It's as if I found a piece of myself that had always been missing.''

Laura winked at her. "That missing piece is Rowe."

The simply spoken words struck home. "When he's around, everything feels right. When he's gone, it's all confused."

"Sounds like you've fallen in love with your husband."

Jenna blinked, startled. "Laura, love doesn't come that fast between a man and woman."

"Love comes in all shapes and sizes. For Matt and me, it came slow. I'd known him since I was eight. When we were kids all we did was fight and bicker. Fact is, I had my cap set for another young man in town when Matt took Rowe's job on my daddy's farm. I'd take lunch out to Matt each day in the field. I didn't think much of his wisecracking manner, and at first, I'd drop the food off and leave. But as the time passed, I started lingering more and more, until one day I looked at him and knew he was the one for me."

"That's how I always figured it would be. It was that way between Everett and me."

"Everett?"

"My former fiancé."

Laura leaned closer to Jenna. "Why didn't you marry him?"

"He didn't want Kate." Jenna sighed. "Laura,

I didn't give birth to Kate. My sister died giving birth to her.''

There were a hundred questions Laura could have asked, but she didn't. "And this fiancé of yours wouldn't take Kate?"

"No."

Laura frowned. "You're not still in love with him, are you?"

"No," she said honestly. The thought of Everett left her cold. The thought of Rowe set her on fire. "I wonder now if I ever really was."

"You couldn't really have loved someone who would turn his back on a child."

Jenna started when the door to the examining room opened and Matt hobbled into the room, leaning heavily on crutches. He had thinned considerably, but was growing stronger every day. "I've had my fill of being poked and prodded."

Doc Carter followed, wiping his hands on a clean cloth. "Stop your bellyaching."

The old doctor's vinegar was nothing but bluster, Jenna realized now. She remembered how he'd worked on Matt, laboring to exhaustion to save the rancher's life, as well as his leg.

Jenna stood and helped Matt to her chair. He winced as he lowered himself onto the wooden seat. "I swear, I'll never complain about hard work again. All this lying about is driving me nuts."

Doc Carter glanced down at Laura's unfinished broth. "Eat! The sooner you two mend the sooner I'll have my clinic back." He walked out of the room and slammed the door behind him.

Matt's gaze swung to the bowl. "Doc's right. You need to take care of yourself and the little one."

Laura's hands slid protectively to her stomach. "Yes, dear." She picked up her spoon and started to eat again.

Satisfied, Matt turned in his chair toward Jenna. "Heard from Rowe?"

Jenna tried to keep all traces of emotion from her face. "No. When the sheriff returned to town he said that Rowe was going after Boone."

"Sounds like him. He'll track that bastard down to the ends of the earth if need be." His eyes hardened. "I only wish I was riding with him."

Laura's face paled. "I don't want you to even think about that. You're staying right here with me."

Matt relaxed the tension that had crept into his face. "I'm not going anywhere, darlin'."

His hand brushed her cheek, and she took it in hers and kissed it. The strong bond between them touched Jenna's heart.

Steady, purposeful steps echoed in the outer office. Doc Carter's voice mingled with another man's deep tones. Jenna barely had time to consider who it might be when the door opened and Rowe strode in.

His gaze locked on her. The room melted away and she was conscious only of him and the rapid beat of her heart.

He seemed to drink in every detail about her. And for an instant, his demeanor softened. Hope swelled inside her even as she noted the dark circles below his eyes and the thick stubble blanketing his hollowed cheeks. Mud caked his boots and snowflakes peppered the shoulders of his range coat and the brim of his hat.

Matt coughed. "Welcome back, Rowe."

Rowe tugged off his hat and shoved back a thick lock of hair that was badly in need of trimming. He tore his gaze from Jenna and shifted it to Matt and Laura.

His stern expression vanished and he grinned as he closed the gap between them. He reached out and offered his hand to Matt, who accepted it easily, as he had a hundred times before. "How are you?"

"Can't complain," Matt said.

Rowe leaned down and kissed Laura's cheek. "I can't tell you how glad I am to see you."

Jenna heard the hitch in Rowe's voice, and her heart went out to him.

Laura beamed. "We can thank you and Jenna for saving us. Doc Carter said it was her quick thinking that kept Matt from bleeding to death."

His eyes swung back to Jenna and locked. "She's full of surprises."

The hidden meeting wasn't lost on Jenna. The air between them crackled, and it took all her courage to hold her ground. "Did you find Boone?"

His eyes narrowed. "No." He turned to Matt. "I tracked him a good hundred miles, but he's crawled under some rock to hide."

Matt rubbed his injured leg. "But he'll be back."

"Count on it. He's not finished with me."

Jenna felt a ripple of unease. "What are you going to do?"

He flexed his fingers. "Wait. Stay alert. And when he returns I'm going to kill him."

"What about Kate and me?"

Rowe frowned. "Jenna, this isn't the time to talk."

On cue, Laura yawned loudly. "It's time I kick you two out. Suddenly, I'm very sleepy."

Matt turned and glanced at his wife. Seeing her raised eyebrow, he nodded. "Rowe, you look like you could use a good meal, and I know Jenna's barely eaten these last few weeks. Take your wife over to the hotel and get something to eat."

Rowe shifted uncomfortably. "I came here straight away and haven't been to see the sheriff yet. I need to give him an update."

Laura waved her hand dismissively. "Donelly can wait. Likely he's gone home for lunch like he does every day at this time."

"Laura and I will watch Kate," Matt offered.

"And if she wakes I'll give her a bottle just like you showed me, Jenna." Laura shooed them away. "Go now, leave."

Backed into a corner, Rowe and Jenna agreed. She reached for her coat, but he took and held it while she slid her arms into the sleeves. With his hand pressed to the small of her back, he guided her out of the office onto the boardwalk. A thick layer of snow crunched under her feet, and thick, plump clouds blanketed the sky.

Moving down the boardwalk, they passed a half-dozen people, who greeted them by name. Several of the women inquired about Laura and Matt, others asked about Kate. Jenna greeted each in turn, talking as if she'd known them a lifetime.

"You've made yourself right at home," Rowe said with a note of impatience.

She paused while he opened the hotel's front door, then went inside. "Everyone's been kind. It's easy to feel at home here." She sighed when she saw how rigid his stance was. "Look, if you'd rather go find the sheriff, I can eat by myself."

His jaw flexed. "No. We'll eat. You've gotten thinner."

"So have you."

Fred Avery, the hotel clerk, waved to them from behind his front desk. "Hey, Miz Jenna! Cora sure did appreciate those herbs you suggested."

"How's she feeling?"

"A world better."

"Glad they helped."

"Rowe, good to have you back," Mr. Avery said. "Any luck with Boone?"

"None."

"You think we've seen the last of him?"

"Nope. Fred, can we get a table?"

"Oh, sure thing. Just pick any one, and Cora will be by before you know it."

The dining room in midafternoon was empty, but Rowe still escorted Jenna to a table in the corner. It didn't have a tablecloth, but was clean enough, as were the utensils.

Rowe took Jenna's coat, his hands lingering only an instant on her shoulders before he removed and draped it over an empty chair. He laid his own coat atop hers, then pulled a chair out and waited for her to sit.

Nervous, Jenna took extra care to adjust the

checkered napkin on her lap. He took the seat across from her, resting his fisted hands on the table.

Anxious to fill the awkward silence between them, she said, "Kate's grown so much in the last two weeks. She can get up on her hands and knees now. She rocks back and forth as if she's ready to crawl, but hasn't quite figured out how to do it."

Rowe's fists loosened slightly. "Good."

"I mixed apple butter into her cereal yesterday and she ate every bite."

"Great."

A sigh shuddered from Jenna. She was babbling like a fool about Kate, when there was so many things that remained unsaid between them. "Look, Rowe, about what happened—"

"Good afternoon!" Cora, a cheery woman with graying hair and a flour-stained apron and calico dress, came to the table then. "Heard you folks was hungry."

Rowe allowed a quick smile. "Afternoon, Cora. What's good today?"

"Got a beef stew that's been simmering all morning. Make your mouth water."

"Good. We'll have two bowls and some of that bread you're famous for."

Cora's grin widened. "Two bowls coming right up, sugar." The old cook touched Jenna lightly on the shoulder. "I told Ida Davis about those herbs you give me. She'll be looking for you later to ask about 'em."

"I'll be glad to talk to her," Jenna said.

"You got yourself a good one, Rowe Mercer," Cora said. "Best hold on to her tight."

"I'm not going anywhere," Jenna said before he could answer.

When Cora had left, Jenna pushed aside the butterflies gnawing at her stomach and met Rowe's gaze. "We need to talk about what happened between us. There's so much that's gone unspoken."

"Jenna, there's nothing to say."

"There's everything to say. It's time I told you about Victoria, Everett, everything that happened in Virginia."

He tossed his napkin on the table and leaned forward. "Jenna, I've done a lot of thinking and I've come to the decision that you're better off without me."

Chapter Fifteen

The ground seemed to shift under Jenna. She folded her hands in her lap, determined to still the panic racing through her. "I am not better off without you."

He gripped the arms of his chair until they creaked under the pressure. "And I want a wife who's suited for life out West. I don't have time to coddle a woman who has no business living out here in the first place."

She swallowed her rising panic. "I'm not leaving, no matter what you say. This is where Kate and I belong."

"You *don't* belong here," he said.

"We are staying." She stared into Rowe's stormy eyes. "I lied to you. That was wrong, but at the time it felt like the only choice I had. My first priority was protecting Kate, and I couldn't chance trusting you—the risk was too great.'' With deliberate slowness she reached for her water glass and took a long, deep drink. The cool liquid slid down her dry throat. ''Now I see how wrong I was.''

''This isn't about the lie, Jenna. It's about you not belonging here—us not suiting.''

''I hurt you.''

He stared at her across the table, his expression hard. ''This isn't the kind of life you deserve.''

''It's the kind of life I want. It's the kind of life that makes me feel alive for the first time in my life.''

Rowe swore. ''Don't you get it? I don't want you.''

Jenna had always avoided conflict—had run from it at times. But she wasn't the same person who had left Alexandria over a month ago. She wasn't running from Saddle Creek or Rowe. She leaned forward. ''Too bad, you've got me.''

He tapped his index finger on the table. ''If it's money you're worried about, don't.'' He reached in his breast pocket and pulled out a folded, crisp piece of paper. He pushed it toward her. ''I've set up an account for you in Denver. It's a fair settlement.''

Jenna unfolded the paper. The sum listed on the sheet was staggering. She and Kate could live comfortably for many, many years. She refolded the paper and pushed it toward him. "I don't want your money."

"Well, it's all you're getting from me."

She pretended not to hear him. "Is this about Boone? The fact that you were a bounty hunter?"

Surprise flickered in his gray eyes. "Who told you?"

"It doesn't matter. I know."

"Then you understand why I'm not right for you."

"Kate and I are returning to the ranch."

"That's the last place I want you two!" He pushed himself to his feet with such force his chair toppled over. "There's a ticket waiting for you at the stagecoach station. I've instructed Pappy to pack your belongings and forward them to Denver. Your stage leaves in the morning."

Rowe strode out of the restaurant, leaving Jenna alone. Crushing defeat weighed on her chest.

Cora sauntered toward the table then, a heaping bowl of stew in each hand. She set the bowls down. "Where's Rowe running to?"

Jenna cleared her throat. "He's been called away."

The older woman propped her hands on her wide hips. "You know folks in town are still talking about you saving Matt and Laura's lives."

"You'd have done the same."

"Of course I would, honey, but I ain't a green-horn, a near stranger to these parts." Cora's plain speaking held no malice, and Jenna didn't take offense. "Nobody around here expected that kind of gumption from you," Cora continued. "Fact is, we all was taking bets that you'd be gone by now."

"If my husband has his way, I'll be gone on the morning stage."

The cheeriness in Cora's smile faded and her eyes narrowed a fraction. "What do *you* want?"

Jenna set her spoon down. "I want to stay. But I don't have the first clue how to manage it."

"He'll be back."

Jenna stared blankly at the food, her appetite gone. "I'm not so sure."

Cora muttered something about men and rocks. "I imagine he's just worried about Boone. Heard tell he hasn't caught up with the rat yet. But he will. Rowe always gets what he wants."

Jenna shifted uncomfortably. "That's what I'm afraid of."

A sly smile curled the edges of Cora's full lips. "The problem is Rowe don't always know *what* he wants. Like all men, he sometimes needs a little coaxing from time to time."

"Coaxing Rowe is like coaxing a mountain." Jenna stirred the spoon in her stew. "I know you must be busy." She prayed the woman would leave, give her time to think of a way to fix her mess of a marriage.

But Cora lingered as if she had all the time in the world and noplace to go. "Even mountains can be toppled with the right about of dynamite."

"I suppose."

"I reckon Rowe'll go over to Sheriff Donelly's and report in."

"I suppose."

"Then I reckon he'll start organizing another search party. He's never been one to give up."

Except on her, Jenna thought miserably.

Cora studied her nails, bitten down to the quick. "Then I reckon he'll go on up to his room here at the hotel. Get himself some shut-eye."

Jenna raised her gaze to Cora's. "I'd forgotten he has a room here."

The woman scooped up Rowe's bowl. "Number six. Stays in the same one every time." She chuckled. "That Rowe, he sure is a creature of habit. My guess is he's already asked Fred to heat a bath for him. He hates trail dust coating his skin."

Jenna nibbled her bottom lip. She rose to her feet, the germ of an idea taking root. The last time she and Rowe had come together in private, emotion had overruled reason. There'd been no planning, no forethought, and the barriers between them had vanished.

Exactly how did a woman wile a man—a very determined man—into her bed?

As if reading her thoughts, Cora said, "I reckon you could use a bath, too."

"I had one this morning."

Cora cocked an eyebrow. "Jenna, you need a bath."

It took an extra moment for the full meaning of Cora's words to sink into Jenna's befuddled mind. When it did, her face split into a wide grin and she hugged the woman. "A bath is exactly what I need."

Cora chuckled. "Atta girl."

Rowe was determined to hold on to his anger. Anger was simple, pure, uncomplicated, and it didn't slice at his insides like sadness and frustration.

He'd spent a frustrating half hour with the sheriff, trying to convince him to raise a new posse. But Donelly hadn't agreed. The weather, the young sheriff had argued, had turned sour and was only going to get worse. Snow already blanketed the countryside. Boone wouldn't be a threat until spring.

Rowe tipped his head forward, using his Stetson

to shield the snowflakes from his face as he strode down the boardwalk.

Donelly was a fool. Boone hadn't gone anywhere. He was out there somewhere close, watching, waiting for the right time to strike. Rowe could feel it in his gut.

Boone would return.

And bring with him Rowe's savage past.

Even when Boone had surfaced, Rowe hadn't been worried at first about the old days. Then the Holts had been shot, their cabin burned, and he'd started to feel like he was sliding into the past. Then days ago, alone on the trail, he'd stopped to water his horse. He'd knelt by the small pond and yanked off his hat, expecting to wash his face, clear his mind. But as he'd dipped his hands into the cool waters, he'd caught sight of his reflection. His face, hard and lined by the sun, was covered in a week's growth of grime. He'd washed it clean, but no amount of washing erased what he'd seen— the soulless bounty hunter who'd tracked and killed more men than he could remember.

His mind had turned to Jenna then—her blue eyes reflecting innocence, her graceful fingers holding a dented tin coffee mug as if it were fine china. The way she carried herself with the poise of a lady.

She didn't belong out here with him. She belonged in a fancy drawing room, where life was safe and tame. He couldn't bear to watch the light being stripped from her eyes by backbreaking work, or to see another rattler like Boone, bent on revenge, gun her down. It wasn't a matter of if, but when one would strike without warning, killing him, or worse, Jenna or Kate.

Better they were out of his life forever, safe, and living in the city, where his past couldn't harm them.

Minutes ago, he'd slipped by the clinic and taken a peek at Kate. The little mite was awake, lying next to Laura on the cot, playing with her socked feet. He'd indulged himself and scooped her up in his arms, pleased and saddened when she'd grinned at him.

Rowe doubted he'd ever get over losing Jenna and Kate, but he loved them too much to cage them in his world.

Now, as he climbed the hotel stairs, his spurs jangled quietly. He reached his room weary and aching, eager to sink into the tub of hot water and drain the bottle of whiskey Fred had promised to have ready for him.

Rowe shoved open the door and strode into the room, dropping his hat on an overstuffed chair. He'd always used room six when he was in town. The room wasn't Fred's fanciest by far, but it was large and enjoyed the morning light. An extra large brass bed nestled close to the double windows.

Hot steam rose from the tub, curling into the air. Soap, a clean towel and a full whiskey bottle sat on a chair next to the tub.

Rowe wasted no time stripping off his jacket and shirt. He unbuckled his guns and hung them on the chair next to the tub, then sat down long enough to pull off his dusty boots and peel off his socks and work pants.

He padded toward the tub and climbed in. Sinking down, he savored the sensation of hot water easing over his tired limbs. He dipped below the surface and let the water lap against his face. He came up for air, shoved his wet hair back with his fingers and set about the task of scrubbing his dirt-caked skin. Finally clean, he picked up the whiskey bottle and gulped down a mouthful before he stretched out his long body and laid his head against the high back of the tub, resting his arms on the rim. The whiskey bottle dangled from his long fingers.

He tried to clear his mind and let the water soothe him, but his thoughts wouldn't let go of Jenna. Memories of his hands on her soft body flooded his senses.

Once again he gulped a mouthful of liquid fire. As he stared at the bottle's label, he wondered how much whiskey it would take to drown out the sweet taste of her lips or to silence the memory of her moans as he'd started to make love to her.

His body hardened thinking about her. Unleashed sexual tension stretched every sinew in his body to the breaking point. He groaned and closed his eyes. How was he ever going to forget Jenna?

Lost in his misery, he almost missed the squeak of the turning doorknob. But he heard it and his senses snapped to attention. Instinct took over. In one fluid move, he snatched his gun from the chair beside him, rose and whirled around, gun cocked.

He nearly stumbled back when he saw Jenna closing his door and locking it. "What the devil are you doing here?"

Without answering, she knelt down and shoved the key under the door. "Locking us in."

"Why the hell would you do that?" Water dripped from his naked body. Despite the chill in the air, his skin burned.

Primly, she removed her cape and hung it next to his coat. "We aren't finished yet."

Just the sight of her made his body hum. "Get out!"

She shrugged as she tugged off her gloves and removed her bonnet. "Can't. I just locked us in."

"Jenna." He packed as much menace as he could into her name, hoping to scare her away.

Instead, she grinned until her gaze slid from his face down his body. He saw shock flash in her blue eyes, but she held her ground. "Are you going to stand there all day, dripping wet, pointing a gun at me?"

He lowered the gun instantly, then snapped up his towel and wrapped it around his waist. "You should never sneak up on a man."

She unfastened the buttons of her fitted jacket and slipped it off to reveal a sheer cotton shirt, with a low, lace-trimmed neckline that skimmed the top of her full breasts. "I couldn't think of any other way to get your attention."

"Get out!" he roared.

Unruffled, she strolled across the room and sat on the edge of the bed. She unlaced her boots and kicked them off.

"What the hell are you doing here?"

She reached for the soap. "Like me to wash your back?"

Despite his best efforts, his gaze dipped to her cleavage. White-hot need singed his gut. He clutched the towel so tightly his knuckles turned white. He understood now what hell on earth was. "No!"

A lazy smile curved her lips. "Then what do you propose we do?"

He vaulted out of the tub, then retreated a step. "How about you leave?"

Jenna closed the distance between them. "No."

"Damn it, I'm trying to be noble."

"I don't want noble, I want my husband." To emphasize her point, she leaned forward, then pressed her lips to his.

A lifetime of self-discipline was put to the test. Water dripping from his body pooled on the wood floor. "I don't want this."

"Yes, you do."

He clenched the towel tighter. "We can't do this. It's not right."

She stared at him for long, tense seconds before she said, "My proud, fierce husband. I always thought you were the unbreakable warrior, but now I see that, like me, you are humbled and frightened by the power that passes between us."

He muttered an oath. "I'm not afraid."

"Then prove it."

"Jenna, this isn't going to happen. You are leaving Saddler Creek."

She tucked a lock of his hair behind his ear. "Scaredy-cat."

He decided then that she'd lost her mind. "*I'm* the one who's acting like the adult here."

"More like a baby if you ask me."

He jerked his head away from her hand and

started to prowl the room. "Why the hell are you doing this to me? I gave you an out. You'll have money. Everything you want. Why push it?"

"I don't have everything I want." Her voice sounded so damn calm, whereas his heart was thundering in his chest.

He stabbed his fingers through his damp hair. "Then tell me what it is you want. I'll get it for you and you can be on your way."

"I want you."

He closed his eyes. The wall around his heart, built brick by brick with pain and sorrow, tumbled. Exposed and vulnerable, he whispered, "You don't want me."

"Yes, I do."

"Jenna, you don't have enough experience to know what you want."

"I know how lonely and lost I felt before I met you. How whole I feel now that I have you."

"It's not that simple." Though he prayed it could be.

"It is."

Her refusal to see the obvious frustrated him. "Life with me is going to be hard and dangerous. I can't protect you from all the dangers. At first I thought I could, then I saw Laura lying unconscious in the dirt, bleeding so badly." The image would haunt him for the rest of his days. "Jenna,

I couldn't live with myself if something like that happened to you."

"I'm a big girl who survived quite a bit before I even met you."

He shook his head, weary of being noble when all he wanted to do was take her in his arms. "You think you've got it all figured out, but you don't understand what you're giving up."

Anger flashed in her sapphire eyes. "You mean like friends that don't speak to me? A fiancé who values his name more than me? Parents who'll never forgive my unpardonable sin of protecting Kate, their own grandchild? So I won't have as many *things* as I did in Virginia. For your information, Mr. Mercer, *things* don't offer solace when you're afraid, or listen to you when you need someone to talk to. *Things* don't make me happy. You make me happy."

"Boone's out there!"

"Boone, Boone, Boone. We'll deal with him and whoever comes our way together, if and when that day comes," she added.

"The day will come, Jenna."

She took Rowe's hand in hers. "Okay. But let's not waste all the days, months or years that stand between us and then. Let's enjoy what we have."

She wrapped her arms around his neck, rising on tiptoe so her lips were close to his. His damp chest soaked her blouse, and he realized she wasn't wearing a corset when he saw the tantalizing curve of her nipple jutting against the thin fabric.

"You came here to seduce me," he growled.

A wicked smile curved her full lips. "I waited in the hallway until I heard you slip into the tub." She nipped his lip with her teeth. "I came in only when I was certain you couldn't escape me."

With one hand still on the towel, he wrapped the other around her waist. "You're not making this easy."

She kissed his chin and then the corner of his mouth. "Good."

"There's no going back, Jenna."

"Even better."

A primitive growl rumbled in his throat. He dropped the towel and crushed her against him. "You deserve better."

"You're more than I ever dreamed of."

He searched her blue eyes. "God help me, but I don't want to let you go."

"Then don't."

He cupped his hand behind her head. "If you had a lick of sense you'd run."

"I'm never running again. Especially from you."

Groaning, he released the reins of control and surrendered to a lifetime of need, wanting and his love for Jenna.

Chapter Sixteen

Jenna leaned into the kiss as Rowe cupped her face in his powerful hands. His tongue slid deeper into her mouth, and the beat of her heart quickened. His touch had the power to drive rational thought from her mind. So she did what came naturally.

Jenna savored the way her senses ignited. She skimmed her fingers up Rowe's broad, slick chest and wrapped her arms around his neck. "Rowe," she whispered.

He crushed her against him. His touch was urgent, as if he were half-starved.

Reeling, she savored his warmth, the hint of whiskey on his lips and the way his masculine scent mingled with the tangy fragrance of the soap he'd used.

She anticipated what was to come. No walls existed between them now, and she was free to lose herself completely in these new, tantalizing sensations.

He groaned and banded his arms around her waist, crushing her against his chest. His kisses made her dizzy with wanting.

At that moment, she reached the limits of her experience, and didn't know what to do next.

Rowe did.

She may have launched this plan of seduction, but he took control of it.

"Touch me," he whispered hoarsely. He took her hand in his and guided it to his erection. "Here."

Her hands trembled as she caressed him. She sensed the power, the need as she stroked the velvet-soft skin.

"Ah, Jenna, you drive me mad."

He scooped his arm under her knees and deftly lifted her off the floor. In three quick strides, he reached the bed and gently lowered her to the mattress. It sank under her weight, then deeper when he straddled her.

Passion burned in his eyes as he cupped her breasts and, with his thumbs, coaxed the pink tips into erect peaks.

Jenna arched her back, pushing into him. His

touch drove bolts of desire through her. She'd never felt so alive, so wanted.

He shoved the blouse from her shoulders, exposing her breasts. Wasting no time, he lowered his mouth to her nipple and suckled.

Jenna hissed in a breath. She grabbed fistfuls of the coverlet as she tried to hold on to the remnants of her sanity.

Rowe dragged his hands over her belly, to stroke the mound between her legs. The sensation was explosive and she arched again.

A wicked smile played on his lips as his face hovered above hers. He stared at her, relishing the desire brewing inside her. He kissed her. There was nothing gentle about the kiss. It was meant to ravish and conquer.

She laced her fingers through his thick mane. Insatiable hunger nipped at her insides. She could feel the moisture between her thighs.

Rowe broke the kiss and rose up on his knees. "I want to see all of you."

He removed her blouse completely, then reached for the buttons trailing down the front of her skirt. His fingers worked quickly, and in seconds he'd peeled away the garments and exposed her naked body.

Her pale skin glistened in the afternoon sunlight that washed over the bed.

Rowe knew loving her might be selfish, but God help him, he couldn't bear to live without her.

He came down on her, searing her with another kiss. The friction of his naked flesh against hers set off a firestorm inside him. He nudged his knee between her legs, spreading them.

Desire sent his blood surging as it never had before. He reached for her center, amazed at how moist she was. She was ready for him and he couldn't wait any longer.

She lifted hips and opened her legs wider. He positioned himself, then, as slowly as he could, pushed inside her.

Jenna closed around him. There was no pain this time, only a delicious tightening, and the throbbing sensation of pent-up desires. Instinctively, she wrapped her legs around him, pulling him deeper.

He started to move inside her and she found herself matching the rhythm, which was as old as time. When his hand slipped between her legs and touched her, she arched, then dropped her head back against the pillow, moaning softly.

"Rowe!"

In one instant she stood on the edge of a cliff, in the next she was tumbling. Over and over the sensations rolled through her. She called out Rowe's name, her voice straining with this first-time pleasure.

Rowe started to move faster, holding on to her as he bucked like a man possessed. Together their pleasure soared, then collided and exploded.

Jenna's body went limp, and Rowe collapsed against her, panting, his body glistening with sweat. The rapid drumbeat of his heart pounding against her breastbone matched her own. She couldn't string two thoughts together, lost as she was in a dewy haze.

As their hearts returned to their normal tempo, he rolled off her, a lazy smile curling his full mouth. He cuddled her body against his and cupped his hand to her breast, nestling his face in the crook of her neck. "Forever and always, Mrs. Mercer."

"Always," she whispered.

Relaxed and satiated, they drifted into a dreamless sleep.

Long shadows etched the rose-papered walls when Jenna woke. She extended her arms in a long, languid stretch. Never had she known such peace.

Rowe nipped her ear. "I was wondering when you'd wake up."

She rolled on her back and stretched again like a contended cat. "Have I slept the afternoon away?"

"Yep." He stared down at her, his eyes darkening with need. He was in no rush to go anywhere.

Jenna dragged her finger down the center of his chest. "We should get dressed. Get moving."

"It would be the responsible thing to do." Rowe stroked her breast and his erection pressed hard against her thigh. To her surprise, her nipple hardened into a peak, and need replaced satisfaction.

She'd expected that they would share a marriage bed. That's what husbands and wives did. But she'd never expected such pleasure, so raw and so freeing.

Her life had been filled with the unexpected ever since she'd met Rowe.

She had vowed during the long months when she'd been utterly alone, abandoned by Everett, that she would never open her heart again. But Rowe's quiet strength had eroded the walls around her heart. She'd expected he would give her safety, security, a new life, but never the chance to love again.

Jenna knew then that she loved Rowe.

She traced her finger the length of the jagged scar that snaked down his cheek, then skimmed the outline of his lips. "I want you again. Inside me."

His eyes darkened with need as he swirled his

fingertip around her nipple. "Whatever the lady wants."

"Is it always like that?"

"Like what?"

"So exciting. So shattering."

"Not always." He kissed her naked shoulder, and his hand slid over her flat belly. "Sometimes it's better."

A throaty laugh rumbled in her throat. "Better just might kill me."

When Jenna woke again, moonlight cast a warm glow on the walls. She stretched out her arms, fully expecting to feel Rowe's long, lean body next to her.

But he wasn't there.

Her jolt of panic was extinguished in an instant by Rowe's voice. He spoke in hushed tones, clearly talking to someone else. Curious, she pushed up on her elbow.

He stood by the window, his body cloaked by shadows just outside the circle of moonlight cascading into the room. A skyful of stars glistened above the endless landscape, now blanketed in snow.

Jenna wondered who he was talking to, until he stepped into the moonlight. He was holding Kate. The baby clung to him, her tiny face staring intently into his as he spoke to her in hushed tones. His warrior's arms rippled with muscles, yet he held the babe as gently as if she were made of glass.

Kate, at ease in Rowe's arms, grabbed his nose with her tiny hand. Jenna heard Rowe's deep chuckle.

"I reckon when a city gal looks up at the stars she sees wishes," he said to the infant. They turned toward the window. "But you're not a city gal anymore and you're gonna need to learn how to read the sky."

Kate grinned.

Holding the sheets to her naked body, Jenna rolled onto her side, careful not to disturb them.

"Learn to read the sky and it'll always lead you home." Rowe pointed to a bright start directly south of town. "See that one, the one between the mountains?"

Kate gurgled.

"You ever get lost, just head toward that star. As long as it's shining between those two peaks, you're headed toward home."

Kate yawned and laid her head on Rowe's shoulder.

He patted the baby on her back. "There's a lot you have to learn, Kate Mercer. But don't you worry about a thing. Your ma and I will be there every step along the way, to make sure you manage.'' Kate drifted off to sleep, her head resting comfortably on Rowe's shoulder.

He held the baby for several minutes before he carefully laid her in her cradle, which he must have brought from the clinic while Jenna slept. He took extra care to tuck Kate's blanket around her tiny body before he stood. For a handful of seconds, he gazed down at her sleeping form.

Jenna was overcome with her love for Rowe. Moments passed before she trusted herself enough to speak. ''How did you manage to get Kate away from Laura? And how'd you get out of the room?''

He turned toward her. ''Spare key in my boot. An odd habit.'' Even in the dim light, she could see his smile. ''Laura didn't put up a fuss when I told her I sleep better when my family is under one roof.''

''Family. That sounds so nice.''

He moved toward the bed, and the mattress sagged under his weight when he sat down. ''It's more than I ever dared wish for.''

She laid her hand on his. ''I wished upon a star once.''

He turned her hand over, traced the lines on her palm with his fingertip. ''And what did you wish for?''

"For one particular boy to kiss me under the mistletoe." She laughed. "I was eleven."

"And the young boy in question—my competition—how old was he?"

"Twelve. His name was Freddie Danvers. He was knocked-kneed and painfully shy, but he was the best chess player and, like me, loved to read books."

Rowe lifted his gaze to hers. "Did you get your wish?"

"Yes. But I was sorry to discover Freddie had a tendency to sweat when he was nervous."

Rowe slid his hand along her leg. "Have pity on the poor boy. Likely he knew he was in over his head."

"Hardly. My love of chocolates had me looking more like a butterball than a girl."

"My guess is Freddie didn't agree. You likely had the lad tongue-tied and hoping he had sense enough to say the right thing."

"What makes you say that?"

"Because you do the same to me."

Her mouth went dry. "You have never been at a loss for words."

He pulled her into an embrace, holding her body close to his. "You make me as nervous as a schoolboy. I can barely talk when I'm around you."

"The mighty Rowe Mercer, a nervous school-boy? That I could never imagine."

"Believe it." He kissed her shoulder. "Those first few days you were in Colorado, I could barely think straight around you, let alone talk. I've never known such long, agonizing nights, lying there beside you, not touching you."

A shudder passed through her body. She wrapped her arms around his neck and drew him closer. "You can touch all you like now."

Boone was determined to endure winter's icy grip. He'd stayed three steps ahead of Rowe Mercer these last two weeks, had driven himself to exhaustion, but he wouldn't quit.

He understood that this was a test of his character designed by his brother, Jimmy.

Boone glanced up at the clouded night sky and imagined Jimmy looking down on him now, watching to see if he had what it took to bring down Rowe Mercer.

Boone clutched the army blanket around his shoulders and leaned against the boulder.

Yes, this was a test.

And he intended to pass.

He wedged his body between two boulders, trying to block the winds that tore at his flesh. There'd be no fire tonight. This close to town, even in a snowstorm, fires would be easily spotted. And he was too near success to mess things up.

His plans hadn't gone as he'd expected. After he'd shot the Holts and burned their house, he'd expected Mercer to come after him, his mind clouded with rage and sorrow. Mercer would have been an easy target. But he hadn't come, and Boone had been forced to rethink his plans.

Failure of his first strategy hadn't dampened his spirits, however. He had outsmarted Mercer twice in the last two weeks by slipping away from the hideout just hours before Mercer and the posse had arrived, leaving the other drunken fools to be captured. Then, before the snowfall had ended, he'd doubled back toward Saddler Creek. With his tracks now covered, no one would realize he'd returned.

"I was smart, Jimmy," Boone said. "I did just like you said. I kept my head. I didn't drink and I doubled back when Rowe gave up."

Don't kid yourself, boy. You screwed up when you didn't finish off the Holts.

Boone winced at the voice in his head. He wanted to do everything just right. To be perfect. "I thought they was dead. They was lying so still, and there was so much blood."

Should've put an extra bullet in their heads just for good measure.

"You're right, Jimmy. If you'd been there it would have been different."

Boone closed his eyes. The pounding in his head was getting worse.

He was so lonely. So confused.

"It'll be different next time. You'll see."

It better be. Mercer's waiting for you. He'll be on guard. You'll only get one more chance.

"I'm going into town tonight." Boone raised his head and looked at the inky sky.

Soon he'd have what Mercer cherished the most.

Chapter Seventeen

A smile tipped the edges of Jenna's mouth as she pushed back the curtains of the hotel room. Sunlight washed over the floor and the bed's rumpled sheets. Her cheeks warmed when she remembered the night she and Rowe had shared.

He'd only been gone five minutes, yet she missed him already. He'd delayed his departure as long as possible, but in the end his search for Boone could no longer be ignored.

She wrapped her arms around her chest, grateful Kate still slept. The extra few minutes alone gave Jenna time to savor her memories.

There'd been no words of love after their love-making, but she didn't need words, she told herself. Rowe's passion for her communicated his feelings better than anything he could have said.

She hummed a light tune as she reached for her

clothes and began to dress. Last night marked a new start for them and filled her with more hope than she'd ever dared wish for.

Life was so good.

The loud knock on the door startled her from her thoughts. She quickly fastened the last few buttons on her bodice, wondering who it could be. Then she saw Rowe's hat on the bed and chuckled. It wasn't like him to be forgetful, but she suspected last night might have knocked him off-kilter as much as it had her.

She scooped up the hat and hurried toward the door. "Your mind is slipping, Mr. Mercer." She flung open the door.

The smile on her face vanished when she saw Boone standing there. He stood with his hat in hand. Grime smeared his tattered coat and pasty skin. He smelled as if he hadn't bathed in months. "Miz Jenna, I've come for you."

Jenna responded by slamming the door. But Boone was too quick. He shoved his foot in the gap, curled his fingers around the edge of the door and shoved it open.

Jenna stumbled back, her first thoughts for Kate. She prayed the infant remained asleep, silent and unnoticed.

"Scream and I'll kill whoever comes through that door," he warned.

Kate, please keep quiet.

Her gaze darted from his piercing eyes to the gun belt slung low on his hip. She had no doubt he'd do exactly as he said. "What do you want?"

He closed the door softly. "You."

She balled her fingers into fists, refusing to let him see them shake. Her mind raced as she remembered what Rowe had told her just before he'd left. He'd be gone no more than an hour. She needed to remain calm, and somehow get Boone away from the baby. "Why me?"

"An eye for an eye." He licked his lips, letting his gaze slither up and down her body. "Your man took the only family I knew, so now I'm doing the same to him. It's only fair."

Jenna swallowed a scream. The tranquil quality of his voice testified to his madness. "I don't want to go with you."

He reached in his pocket and pulled out a hand-rolled cigarette and a match. In no rush to answer, he struck the match against his boot, then raised it to the cigarette's tip. He inhaled twice before he looked up at her through the cloud of smoke. "I ain't asking, I'm telling."

She retreated a half-dozen steps until she bumped into the bedpost. Her proximity to the bed conjured images she didn't dare entertain, and she moved away from it as if scalded.

He strode toward her and for an instant she couldn't breathe. "Get your coat. We're leaving."

"We'll never get out of town without people seeing us."

"Got a covered wagon out back. No one will know you're in it."

Her hands did tremble this time. "Rowe will follow us."

"I'm counting on it." Boone tossed the cigarette on the floor and ground it out with the tip of his boot. Then, without warning, he drew back his fist and slammed it into her jaw. Her mind registered pain and shock before she tumbled into unconsciousness.

"What do you mean, Boone's doubled back?" Rowe's voice ricocheted off the adobe jailhouse walls as he glared at Sheriff Donelly.

The younger man shifted uneasily in his chair. "Ran into a couple of cowhands in the saloon last night. They said they saw Boone a few days back—ten miles outside of town, near Squibb's Lake."

Rowe planted his fists on the sheriff's desk and leaned forward. "Why the hell didn't you tell me?"

"I came by the hotel. The clerk said you wasn't supposed to be disturbed."

Rowe straightened, praying for patience. "How fast can you get a posse together?"

"An hour."

"We'll meet out front at noon sharp."

"Rowe, you're getting worked up over nothing."

Rowe paced the floor. "Don't underestimate him."

"You're tied up in knots. Stop borrowing trouble. Go to the hotel and visit with your wife—it'll settle your nerves."

A nagging unease grated down his spine. She'd be up by now, dressed and tending to Kate. "Something about this doesn't feel right."

"Just nerves, Rowe. See Jenna. You'll feel better."

"Yeah, you're right."

As he strode outside, he scowled at the snowflakes drifting down. The sooner he found Jenna the better.

The sun was high overhead when Jenna woke. She lay on her side on a hard wood floor, curled on her side. Her entire body ached and coldness had seeped into her bones. Her teeth chattered despite the protection of her cape.

She pushed herself up and her head started to spin. Gingerly, she touched her jaw and winced.

The cabin was crude and small. There was a cold potbellied stove in the corner, two broken chairs and a pallet.

Boone squatted in the corner of the dingy room, his hands dangling over his knees. "Was beginning to wonder if you'd wake up."

"Where's Kate?"

"Safe...for now."

Panic choked Jenna. *"Where is she?"*

Boone pushed himself up to a standing position. "I ain't telling."

Unspeakable images flashed in Jenna's mind and blocked her ability to reason. "Tell me where she is, you bastard!"

Boone crossed the room and grabbed a fistful of her hair. "Jimmy wanted me to kill you right off. I said no. I said you was special." He drew his gun and shoved the point into the base of her skull. "Now, I'm thinking maybe he was right. That I should have killed you back at the hotel."

Rowe burst through the front doors of the hotel, ignoring the guests who waited to be checked in, and stormed up the main staircase. Kate's distressed cry greeted him when he reached the top landing.

Running now, he stopped short when he reached

his room and saw that the door was ajar. His hand shook when he shoved it open.

Cora sat on the bed, cradling a fussy Kate. Relief washed over her pale face when she saw him. "I just found her, crying her little lungs out."

"Where is Jenna?"

Cora frowned. "I thought she was with you."

He shoved his fingers through his hair. "No. I went by the sheriff's office. I told her I'd be back in an hour."

"That's not like her."

Rowe's mind raced, refusing to let fears take root. But when he saw the cigarette ground into the rug, he swallowed, barely able to breathe.

Boone *had* doubled back!

He'd been here and he had Jenna. "Take the baby to Laura. She'll look after her."

"Where you going?"

"To find my wife."

A surreal calmness overtook Jenna. She didn't want to die. Not when she had a child to raise. Not when it meant leaving Rowe, or never telling him that she loved him so completely.

Love had eluded her most of her life. Now she had more than she'd ever dreamed possible, and she was about to lose it. The sudden insight stirred something in her. Fury, righteous indignation—

whatever it was, it gave her courage. "Jimmy was wrong!" she shouted.

Boone twisted her hair tighter. "Don't say that! He's always right."

She winced and cried out. "Jimmy was wrong about you. You are smarter than he is. Don't let him run your life."

He ground the gun into her flesh. "Jimmy is the best brother."

"Yes, but he never understood how clever you are." Boone was insane, and she felt as if she were walking on eggshells, not sure if her words would calm or enrage him. "He doesn't see how much you have to offer." She moistened her lips. "Think back. There had to be times when you didn't agree with him."

The sound of her heartbeat mingled with his ragged breaths.

"There was a time in Abilene. We was nearly hanged for bank robbery. Jimmy thought it was funny having the posse chase us. It wasn't."

Tears welled in her eyes. "I'm sure it was awful."

Boone eased his hold a fraction. "I started to cry. Jimmy laughed."

"He shouldn't have done that. You were right to be afraid."

Tense seconds passed, then he shoved her away

from him and backed off. He pressed his body against the wall and squeezed his eyes shut.

Jenna slowly rose. Her head throbbed and her legs wobbled, forcing her to lean against the wall herself to maintain her balance.

Boone looked up at her, the desperate hopefulness of a child in his eyes. "I'll let you live. But you gotta do something for me."

She pushed back the wave of nausea that threatened to bring her to her knees. "What?"

"Help me kill Rowe."

Rowe's hunter instincts kicked into play as if he'd never left his bounty hunting days behind.

He crouched near the faint wheel ruts imbedded in the snow. The impressions had started behind the hotel and led away from Saddler Creek toward the mountains. A wagon was the perfect way to smuggle a woman out of town, and the grooves weren't deep, indicating a light cargo.

Jenna.

Rowe squinted as he stared off toward the horizon. There wasn't any sign of life, but he remembered an abandoned lineman's shack tucked into the foothills by the river. The old cabin hadn't been used for a couple of seasons, but he'd seen it this past spring and knew it remained sturdy. A good place to hide.

He rose and mounted his horse. Gripping the reins, he willed his body to relax.

Jenna was going to be fine. She was going to be fine.

Last night he could have opened his heart to her and he hadn't. He prayed it had hadn't been his last chance.

A chill careened down Jenna's back. She stared into Boone's eyes. Cold eyes. Tortured eyes. The eyes of a madman.

Stalling, she tucked her feet under her skirt. "I'm cold. Can we light a fire?"

He shook his head. "Mercer will see the smoke."

Jenna shivered. "Isn't that what you want?"

"Yes," he said warily.

"Then let's not make it so hard for Rowe to find us." Boone was no match for Rowe. When Rowe found her, he'd find a way to rescue her. But she had to stay alive until he arrived.

Boone studied her for tense seconds before he strode over to the small potbellied stove. He shoved kindling into the opening and lit a match. Soon a fire crackled and hissed. The meager flames provided little warmth, but Jenna prayed Rowe would spot the tendrils against the cloudy sky.

The gunman's oily gaze made her skin pucker

with disgust, but she kept her hands steady, out-
stretched in front of the flames. She summoned the
calmest voice she could muster. "Where is the
baby?"

"Safe."

"Where?" The desperation nearly choked her.

"Just safe."

Not knowing where her child was tortured her
more than the cold or Boone's threats. "Rowe will
be here soon," she said. Just saying the words
calmed her racing heart.

Boone grinned. "The sooner the better."

Rowe reached the ridge above the cabin thirty
minutes later. From the rise, he saw the wagon
hidden in a stand of brush and Boone's horse teth-
ered nearby.

Rowe gave a silent prayer of thanks. "Hang on,
Jenna."

He shoved tender emotions aside, determined
not to rush this last leg of his journey. He'd seen
too many men die when they'd given in to anger
and fear.

He left his horse on the far side of the ridge and
traveled the last half mile on foot. Boone might be
crazy but he wasn't stupid. And if Rowe were going to best him, he needed surprise on his side.

Gun drawn, he moved like the Indians, low and

quiet, toward the cabin, then crouched by the single window. He rose slowly and peered through the smudged panes. A single lantern spat out enough light to illuminate the interior.

Jenna sat in the far corner, her feet tucked under her body, her head bowed. Even at this distance he could see that she was shivering. But she was alive, and that was all that mattered.

Boone sat in the opposite corner. His eyes were closed, his pistol cocked and ready.

Rowe sank down and moved around to the front of the cabin. He paused long enough to cock his pistol, then, with a savage kick, charged through the door.

The barest hint of shock registered on Boone's face before he raised his pistol and shot wildly, missing Rowe.

Rowe heard a weak cry from Jenna, but his gaze didn't waver. He fired twice. Both bullets caught Boone square in the chest.

Rowe strode over to him, nudged him twice with his boot. Only when he was certain that he was dead did he turn to Jenna.

His knees nearly buckled when he saw her slumped against the wall, a blossom of blood staining her shoulder. She looked up at him, her eyes wide with shock. "I knew you'd come."

"Jenna, we've got to get you to town."

She gripped his arm when he tried to lift her. "Where's Kate?"

"Home safe."

She smiled, then passed out against his chest.

During the ride back to town, Jenna was aware only of two things—the pain burning her shoulder, and Rowe cradling her in his arms.

Once they arrived, he wasted no time getting Jenna into Doc Carter's office. When he laid her on the cot, she focused on his soothing whispers and his featherlike touch.

The next thing Jenna remembered was waking up out of a deep sleep. She felt as if she were clawing her way to the surface of a deep, murky pond. When her eyes fluttered open, Rowe was there. Dark shadows marred the skin under his eyes and a thick growth of beard blanketed his square jaw. He looked as if he hadn't slept in days.

He brushed the hair off her forehead. "I was wondering when you'd finally wake up."

"Where's Kate?"

Rowe nodded toward the cradle in the corner. "Sleeping. Waiting for her mother to wake up, just like the rest of us."

Jenna's mouth felt like it was full of cotton. "How long have I been asleep?"

"Two days." Rowe straightened his shoulders.

"Doc said the sleep would help you mend. Boone shot you in the arm. There was a lot of blood. A fever. I was afraid we'd lose you."

She squeezed his hand. "I told you I'm not going anywhere."

He nodded, shifted and pressed his lips to her hand. "I should have been there to protect you and I wasn't. I failed you."

She brushed his cheek with her fingers. "You saved me."

He swallowed. "Boone didn't hurt you, did he?"

She understood his meaning. "No."

"I've never been so afraid."

"I was scared, too, but what was worse was knowing I'd never told you that I love you."

His gaze probed hers like a dagger. "Jenna."

"Knowing I'd be leaving Kate and you behind kept me strong."

He kissed her hands. "God, Jenna, I love you so much."

A slow grin touched her lips. "As I remember, Mr. Mercer, you said something about babies in the summer."

Epilogue

Matthew David Holt, Jr.'s delivery was unusually quick, but he was a healthy weight and equipped with a set of robust lungs.

Jenna carried the young Master Holt into the sitting area of the Holts' new house, where Matt sat in a chair next to Rowe and Kate.

Matt jumped to his feet, tipping his chair over, and ran to Jenna. "How's Laura?"

Jenna smiled. "She's wonderful. Sleepy, but fit as a fiddle. Come meet your son."

"Son!" Gingerly, he peeled back the blanket with a trembling hand and looked at the sleeping infant. "He's got ten fingers and toes?"

Jenna grinned. "Your son has all his pieces and parts in the right places."

He kissed the newborn, tears streaming down his face. "I'm going to peek in on Laura."

"She's waiting for you."

Matt hurried off, leaving the babe with Jenna. Rowe rose then and, with Kate in his arms, strode toward Jenna. Kate clung to her father as she peered at the babe in her mother's arms. "Baby."

Jenna grinned. "That's right. Baby."

"He's fit?" Rowe said, studying him closer.

"He's perfect."

"Good. He'll need to be quick to keep up with our Kate."

Jenna's cheeks warmed. "And her little brother or sister."

Rowe's gaze locked on her. "What are you saying?"

She grinned. "The next Mercer won't be here by summer—more like late fall."

Rowe wrapped his arm around her and, careful not to hurt the babies, kissed her fiercely on the lips. When he drew back she was breathless and a little light-headed. "I love you, Jenna."

"Biscuits and all?" she teased.

"Biscuits and all, darlin'."

* * * * *

Do Westerns drive you wild?
Then partake of the passion and adventure
that unfold in these brand-new stories from
Harlequin Historicals

On sale July 2002

THE TEXAN by Carolyn Davidson
(Texas, 1880s)
*A U.S. Marshal and an innocent spinster
embark on the rocky road to wedded bliss!*

THE BRIDE'S REVENGE by Anne Avery
(Colorado, 1898)
*An overbearing husband gets more than he bargained
for when his feisty bride demands her independence!*

On sale August 2002

BADLANDS LAW by Ruth Langan
(Dakota Territory, 1885)
*Will an honor-bound sheriff be able to choose
between his job and his devotion for a woman
accused of murder?*

MARRIED BY MIDNIGHT by Judith Stacy
(Los Angeles, 1896)
*In order to win a wager, a roguish businessman
weds a love-smitten family friend!*

 Harlequin Historicals®
Historical Romantic Adventure!

New York Times Bestselling Author

Stephanie Laurens

Four in Hand

The Ton's most hardened rogues could not resist the
remarkable Twinning sisters. And the Duke of Twyford
was no exception! For when it came to his eldest ward,
the exquisite Caroline Twinning, London's most
notorious rake was falling victim to love!

On sale July 2002

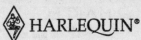

HARLEQUIN®

Is he tall, dark
and handsome...
Or tall, dark
and *dangerous?*

Men of Mystery

**Three full-length novels of romantic suspense
from reader favorite**

GAYLE
WILSON

Gayle Wilson "has a good ear for dialogue and
a knack for characterization that draws
the reader into the story."
—*New York Times* bestselling author Linda Howard

**Look for it in June 2002—
wherever books are sold.**

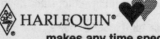

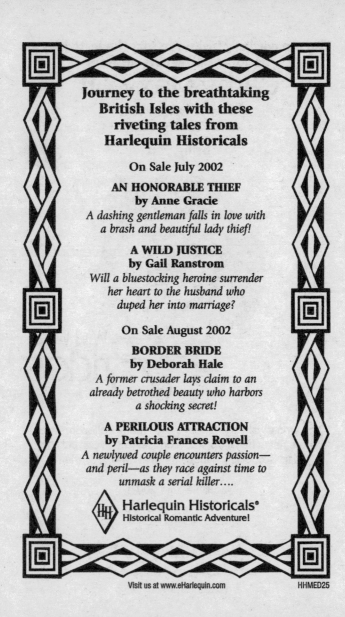